TAKEN IN

Erica Abbott

BELLA
BOOKS

2017

Bella Books, Inc.
P.O. Box 10543
Tallahassee, FL 32302

Printed in the United States of America on acid-free paper.

First Bella Books Edition 2017

Editor: Medora MacDougall
Cover Designer: Judith Fellows

ISBN: 978-1-59493-552-7

Other Bella Books by Erica Abbott

Acquainted with the Night
Certain Dark Things
Desert Places
Fragmentary Blue
One Fine Day

Acknowledgments

As always, concepts for novels come from everywhere around me. For this book, I'd like to thank the following people who provided me with encouragement, ideas, and/or a kick in the writer's pants as needed: MJ, Ann &Amy, Karin Kallmaker, Polly and Kathy. A special thank you for the eye of my turbocharged editor Medora who apparently misses nothing.

I remain grateful to Linda Hill at Bella Books for publishing these stories and to my fellow Bella authors who have been such a joy to me. My readers are the reason I write and I am thankful for you. And for those of you who can't go home, I hope you will find your safe place.

About the Author

Erica Abbott writes romance and romantic suspense because love is the best experience she can imagine. She is a retired attorney and college professor. In addition to reading voraciously, she enjoys bridge, music of all kinds, movies, dogs, and sometimes golf. She lives in beautiful Colorado.

Dedication

To my love, always and forever.

CHAPTER ONE

Until she saw the stranger standing by her front door, Alex Ryan thought it was going to be a relaxing Saturday.

She'd already done the morning's errands: oil change on her car and picking up the dry cleaning on the way home. Most of it was CJ's clothing, as always. Alex's wardrobe tended toward machine-washable cottons. CJ preferred silks, wool, cashmere, and other hard-to-care-for fabrics, the byproduct, Alex supposed, of growing up with a lot of money.

Now it was time for a shower and lunch with friends. A day off with CJ was always worth looking forward to—but the man standing in front of the closed door of the condo she shared with CJ produced a jolt of alarm.

The stranger was broad but not tall. He wore a black suit that didn't fit him very well. The pants were too long, the jacket pulled too tightly across his thick shoulders. He was pacing a few steps up and down the hall, but he stopped when he spotted Alex.

More than twenty years as a cop had trained Alex to make quick assessments of people. This man looked wary but not overtly hostile. More importantly, as far as Alex could tell, he wasn't armed. The tightness of that jacket made it hard to miss a hidden gun.

He had a shaved head and it gleamed in the overhead light. He turned his stout body toward Alex as she approached, blocking the entrance to the condo.

"We're busy," he announced. "Go away."

What the hell? Alex's anxiety ratcheted up another notch.

She stopped a few feet away, too far for him to jump her without a chance for her to escape. "Who are you?" she demanded.

"It don't matter. The lady don't want to be disturbed. Now go away."

The lady? He couldn't mean CJ. Keeping her eyes on him, Alex carefully laid the dry cleaning down on the polished wood floor so it wouldn't wrinkle. She reached into her bag.

She pulled out a leather wallet and held it up to him. Her shield was on one side, her photo identification on the other.

"I'm Captain Alex Ryan, Colfax PD. This is my condominium and I'm going inside. Move away from the door."

He peered at her badge, looking back at her face. She could see him trying to match an ordinary, average-looking, middle-aged woman with the title of police captain. She gave him a moment to think about things since it seemed to be taking him a long time.

She said, "You've got two choices. You can leave the building now or you can tell me what's going on. Either option, you're getting out of my way."

Alex watched him tighten his shoulders. For a second she prepared for a swing at her head. She moved her feet apart a little, shifted her weight onto the balls of her feet, ready to move.

She saw the moment of indecision, the second of disbelief. The next minute she relaxed as his shoulders sagged and his hands dropped.

"My boss, she's inside. She don't want nobody to bother them."

"Who is your boss?"

He shrugged. "Dunno. I'm a driver. Picked her up this morning at the Hilton. She told me to keep anybody away. Gave me a hundred bucks. Dunno her name." He eyed Alex again, clearly disgruntled at the turn events had taken. "She didn't tell me there was gonna be cops."

Alex wondered how many priors he had. Using her best authoritative tone she demanded, "Give me your identification."

He frowned but dug his wallet out. Alex slipped his commercial driver's license from the plastic case, kept it and handed the wallet back to him.

"Okay, Mr. Davis. Go downstairs and wait in your car. I'll be sending your client down in a while."

He stared longingly at the card still in her fingers. "I gotta have my license."

"Behave yourself and I'll send it down with her. Now leave."

He shook his gleaming head. "She ain't gonna like that."

"I suppose not. Good-bye, Mr. Davis."

Defeated by higher authority, he rumbled down the elegant hallway, looking as out of place as overalls at a black-tie dinner.

Alex waited for the elevator doors to close behind him before she picked up the dry cleaning again. She took a couple of breaths to help clear the adrenaline thrumming through her veins. But she was still keyed up from the encounter as she unlocked the front door and went inside.

She hung the dry cleaning in the front closet of the foyer. She didn't know who was visiting CJ, but she was beginning to have an inkling.

"I'm home," she called out.

She saw CJ first, sitting on the sofa. Sitting wasn't really the right description, Alex thought. CJ was perched on the edge of the leather couch, as if she were preparing to flee at any moment. She was staring at someone Alex couldn't see in the easy chair.

Alex stepped into the large living room. CJ had owned the condo when they met, but Alex left her small house and moved in happily soon thereafter. She loved the size of the rooms—and the lack of yard work. In the years they'd been married, Alex had grown to think of the condo as their home together. The mystery novels Alex loved were neatly on the shelves beside CJ's poetry and biographies. Alex's favorite jazz music was playing softly on the sound system in the corner.

Alex knew every inch of the room. But she didn't know the woman who was staring at her angrily from the chair.

Their visitor was meticulously dressed in a linen dress and suit jacket. Her low beige pumps were the exact shade of the purse that sat on the floor beside her. The hands that lay in her lap had several rings, including a large diamond in an old-fashioned setting on her left ring finger.

Alex took in the age spots on the hands and the ropy muscles of her neck to estimate her age. Perhaps seventy? Alex had trouble guessing because the woman had the kind of well-preserved skin, hair, and nails that only money and a determined attention to self-care could accomplish. Her fingernails looked newly done, a light pink polish that didn't call too much attention to her manicure. Her pale skin looked as if it had never seen sunlight and she was carefully made-up, not too much rouge. The only jarring notes in her appearance were the scowl on her face and the choice she—or her stylist—had made for her hair color. It was aggressively red, no longer a color found in nature, although Alex supposed it was highly effective at covering the gray.

Even from halfway across the room, Alex could see that her eyes were a bright shade of green, a color with which Alex had intimate familiarity.

Alex could not have been more astonished if the Easter Bunny had suddenly materialized.

"Mrs. St. Clair, I presume." She greeted the woman who had to be CJ's mother.

"Apparently the man is too stupid to follow the simplest of instructions," she answered tartly. "Whoever you are, this is a private conversation." She had a raspy voice, more a betrayal of her age than her appearance. Alex wondered if she'd ever been a smoker.

Alex turned her gaze to CJ, who finally seemed to regain her ability to speak. CJ stood and walked to Alex's side. She said, "Mother, this is Alex. My wife."

CJ rarely referred to her as a wife, usually preferring "partner," but Alex knew CJ was making a point to a woman she hadn't seen in a very long time. By Alex's count, it had been more than a decade since Lydia St. Clair had seen or spoken to her daughter. *So what are you doing here now?*

"I don't care who you are," Lydia St. Clair answered crisply. "I'm having a private conversation with my daughter. Please leave."

"Mama," CJ cut in sharply. "She's not leaving. This is her home too."

"I doubt that." She gave Alex a probing look. "I imagine your money paid for all of it. Or more precisely, your grandfather's money."

Alex had just a moment to make a choice. She'd never had to face a hostile parent with an announcement that she was gay. Her mother had died of cancer when Alex was ten years old, and her father had died on the job when she was nineteen. She hadn't been able to come out to herself until just a few years ago.

Falling in love with CJ had changed the world for her. For the first time, Alex was happy. They'd been through a lot together, but CJ meant everything to her.

And now this stranger, CJ's mother, was here making CJ look both angry and frightened at the same time. Alex wasn't having that, but she wasn't going to fight either. It would only upset CJ more than she was already.

Alex said calmly, "May I offer you something, Mrs. St. Clair? We finished the morning coffee, I'm afraid, but I'm happy to brew another pot. Or would you prefer something cold? We have iced tea or I think there's lemonade still in the fridge."

CJ turned to her with an expression just short of astonishment. Alex smiled at her.

"No, thank you," Mrs. St. Clair said through tight lips. "This is not a social occasion."

Alex led CJ back to the couch and sat next to her. "No, I'm sure you wouldn't have taken the time to travel from Georgia after all this time for a social call. Please tell us what you need." She took CJ's hand and settled in for the conversation.

Mrs. St. Clair shifted unhappily in the chair and Alex couldn't suppress a flutter of satisfaction. There was only so much a Southern woman could do in the face of a courteous response. Alex had her outmaneuvered.

CJ gripped her fingers firmly. Alex could feel anxiety—and gratitude—in her touch.

Mrs. St. Clair began abruptly. "If your father were still alive, I wouldn't have to be here."

Alex felt rather than saw CJ's flinch. Her father had died a couple of years ago. Mrs. St. Clair had sent word through CJ's trustee that his daughter would not be welcome at the funeral.

CJ found her voice. "What is this about, Mama? Do you need money?"

Mrs. St. Clair straightened her back as if preparing for an assault. Alex couldn't imagine what the hell was going on, but all of her instincts were on high alert.

"It's your brother," Mrs. St. Clair said at length.

"Clayton? Is he sick?" CJ asked.

"No. He's been arrested."

"Arrested?" CJ exclaimed. "For what?"

"He's been charged with murder."

CHAPTER TWO

"Well?" Mrs. St. Clair said into the stunned silence. "Haven't you anything to say?"

"Did he do it?" CJ rasped.

The color rose on Mrs. St. Clair's face. "What an absurd question! Not that I should expect anything different from you, I suppose. Of *course* he didn't do any such thing!"

"But he's been arrested. Charged by the district attorney. And arraigned by now, I imagine."

"Yes, but he pleaded not guilty. It's all a ridiculous mistake."

CJ shook her head. "Probably not."

"What on earth…"

"I'm a police officer, Mama."

Mrs. St. Clair's lips tightened again in what Alex was beginning to realize was a signature expression.

"Yes, I'm aware of that."

"Well, just to let you know. Cops usually get it right. Not always, but almost always. If Clayton's been charged, there are some really good reasons for it."

"It's ridiculous," her mother repeated. "The local police have some sort of vendetta against him."

To Alex's astonishment, CJ broke into a bitter laugh.

"Really, Mama? Since when does the Savannah Police Department take up vendettas against well-to-do white orthodontists?"

Mrs. St. Clair stirred again in her seat. Alex thought she'd never seen anyone so uneasy in an easy chair.

"There's no reason for you to be unpleasant about this situation," she snapped. "Your brother needs your help. He's been unjustly accused."

"If he has been unfairly accused, I presume his lawyer will be addressing the situation. I'm sure he has the best defense attorney your money can buy."

Their visitor finally seemed to find a comfortable position. It appeared to Alex that she was only at ease if CJ was uncomfortable. Alex wanted to order this unpleasant woman out of their house, out of their lives. Send her back to the oblivion she had been in before this morning.

"We hired Miller Ross from Atlanta," she said. "But I can tell he's concerned about the case. He suggested we get a private investigator to see what we could discover to prove that Clayton is innocent."

CJ said sharply, "You don't have to prove he's innocent. The prosecution has to prove he's guilty. All the defense has to do is raise reasonable doubt."

"You don't seem to understand the situation," Mrs. St. Clair said irritably. "This has been in the news, in the papers. Everyone knows about Clayton. 'Prominent Savannah Dentist Arrested for Murder,' that sort of thing. It won't be enough for him just to be found not guilty. It's imperative to prove that he's innocent."

CJ lifted her hand to stop the flow of words.

"All right, Mama. But what do you want me to do about it? I asked you before if you needed money. Is that it?"

"We don't need money. Your brother needs you."

CJ snorted. "For what? Moral support? I haven't talked to him in years."

"Don't be absurd. He needs for you to investigate the case, show where the police got it wrong."

Alex shook her head, unwilling to participate in the discussion between mother and daughter but unable to completely suppress her reaction. CJ shot her a warning look, then said flatly, "Mama, even if it would do you any good, I can't just drop everything and come. I have a job, responsibilities."

"He's your only brother, Belle. There's no reason to turn your back on Clayton."

Other than the fact that he's refused to have any relationship with her because she's a lesbian, Alex thought grimly.

CJ took a long breath. Finally she said, "I'm not promising you anything. I can't just leave. But tell us what happened. Who is the victim?"

Mrs. St. Clair lifted her hands from her lap and laid them on the arms of the chair. Alex could see her fingers digging into the leather. *Uh-oh.*

After a long time she responded, "It was Amy. Someone shot her and they think it was Clayton."

CJ was on her feet in an instant. "Amy? His *wife* Amy?"

"Ex-wife," Mrs. St. Clair corrected her. "They've been divorced for years."

CJ was pacing now. "Oh my God! Poor Amy. I can't believe it. And…oh, Mama! What about Laura?"

"Well, naturally she's very upset, losing her mother and having these terrible accusations leveled at her father."

CJ thrust her fingers through her hair.

Alex risked a question. "I've forgotten how old your niece is. A teenager?"

Mrs. St. Clair answered, "She's fifteen. I'm surprised Belle has even mentioned the girl."

Alex couldn't help herself. "Why wouldn't she? CJ sends her a birthday card and a Christmas present every year."

Mrs. St. Clair opened her mouth and closed it again with a snap. *Ah, didn't know that, did you? Maybe your son has kept some secrets from you.*

"The best thing you can do for Laura, Belle, is clear her father of this absurd accusation."

CJ stopped pacing and sat down again on the couch next to Alex. She leaned forward, elbows on her thighs, and looked intensely at her mother.

"You keep telling us how ridiculous the charge is, but you haven't told us what happened."

The lips returned to their firm line. Alex could see the fine wrinkles appearing around her mouth. Her carefully applied lipstick was just bleeding into the lines. *She must have been truly desperate to come here*, Alex realized suddenly. *She's more than just angry. She's terrified.*

Mrs. St. Clair took a moment. She returned her hands to her lap in an effort to regain her composure.

CJ didn't move. Alex studied her profile. Her eyes were locked on her mother, her brows drawn in slightly in an expression Alex had often seen before—in the department's interview rooms.

"Tell me what happened to Amy," CJ said in a surprisingly soft voice. Alex had already figured out that CJ must have known Clayton's first wife. She did the math. Clayton was already married when CJ left home.

"She was leaving a meeting, at her church. She was walking out to her car when it happened."

"Alone?"

"No. It was after dark. She was walking out with a friend, another woman."

"All right. So we have a witness. What did she say happened?"

The restless shifting resumed. "A man appeared out of nowhere, she said. He demanded Amy's purse. Then he shot her and ran away."

"And the witness identified Clayton?"

Mrs. St. Clair shook her head. "No, she never saw his face. He was wearing a hood or something over his head."

She stopped and CJ waited.

Finally she continued, "They thought it was a robbery, of course. But the next day they found Amy's purse in a trash can near the church. It hadn't been touched. So then they decided that the robbery was a pretext. They arrested Clayton."

Alex said dryly, "I doubt it was quite that simple."

Mrs. St. Clair shot her an unpleasant look, but CJ said, "She's right. What are you leaving out?"

She capitulated with poor grace.

"They found a hooded jacket similar to the one the robber used at Clayton's home. And they found…the gun."

CJ jerked upright. "The murder weapon? Clayton had the gun?"

"He didn't *have* it," her mother corrected her imperiously. "They found it. It was probably put there by the police."

Alex and CJ exchanged a look. Alex said, "It's possible, but that means that they found it somewhere else and decided to frame your son. Why would they do that?"

"They must have had a reason." She sounded uncertain.

CJ shook her head. "That's not going to work, Mama. Where was the gun?"

"In his car."

"Fingerprints?"

"Apparently not. But they verified that it was the gun that killed Amy."

"They've been divorced for years," CJ pointed out. "What do they think his motive was?"

Her hands went back to the arms of the chair. *This won't be good*, Alex thought.

"Money." She half-whispered the word.

CJ looked confused. "Money? How would Amy's death… wait. Insurance?"

Mrs. St. Clair nodded. "The divorce required both of them to carry policies with the other as beneficiary. For Laura's benefit, of course."

"How much?" Alex interjected.

"Five hundred thousand dollars."

"That's a lot of motive. But only if Clayton needed the money," CJ said. "Did he?"

"No! Of course not. Well, not really. His practice is going well, but he had a lot of expenses. Child support, of course, and there were the payments to his ex-wives."

"He was still paying Amy?" CJ asked in surprise. "Property settlement? Or spousal support?"

Mrs. St. Clair sighed. "Just before the divorce, Amy had been diagnosed with MS. The court ordered support for her and Laura both. And of course, he was still paying off Paula and in the middle of the divorce with that Missy."

Alex made an involuntary noise and CJ shot her another warning look.

"I didn't realize he was on his third divorce," CJ said tartly.

"I told him not to marry her," Mrs. St. Clair said with asperity. "She had no breeding. It was always clear to me that she was just after his money."

"Which you say he's running short of," CJ pointed out.

That earned her a glare.

"It's absurd to think that Clayton would kill his daughter's mother for some money," she announced. "He didn't do it, and someone is trying to make it look as though he did. That's why he needs your help, Belle."

CJ sighed. "I told you, Mama, I have a job. I can't just leave."

"You want your brother to go to prison?" Her voice rose imperiously. "What kind of ungrateful daughter are you?"

Alex felt her temper rise as a tight ball in her stomach. She stood up and said, "You're staying at the Hilton, your driver said. We'll be in touch."

Now her mouth twisted in anger. "This is none of your…"

CJ said, "She's right, Mama. I need some time. I'll call you. We need to go. We have lunch with friends."

Mrs. St. Clair gathered her purse and got to her feet. "I'm leaving," she announced as if it were her idea, "but I expect you to call me today, Belle."

CJ simply nodded. She looked exhausted and a bit shell-shocked. Alex said to her, "I'll walk your mother out."

In the foyer, Mrs. St. Clair turned to Alex. "I have something to say to you, so listen carefully. I meant what I said before. I don't want you interfering with this in any way. This is family business and none of your concern. So I will not have you exercising whatever…influence you may have on my daughter to prevent her from helping her brother."

She turned and put her hand on the doorknob.

Alex said, "Wait a minute."

Mrs. St. Clair turned back, her brows drawn together. Her mouth was so firmly set that her lips were scarcely visible.

"I met you for the first time a few minutes ago," Alex said. "In that time, you've tried to keep me out of my own home, exclude me from a conversation concerning my wife and implied that I'm some kind of gold digger who married your daughter for her money. So I got the message. Now you can listen carefully to me. CJ is a woman of good judgment who will make her own decisions. I'm going to support whatever she decides to do. My only agenda is this: if you want CJ's help, treat her with kindness. She deserves nothing less from you."

"I am her *mother*. Who do you think *you* are?"

Mrs. St. Clair's glower was meant to intimidate, but Alex refused to flinch. She wondered how this imperious woman could be the mother of her kind, openhearted partner.

Alex responded, "Let me be clear about who I am. I am the woman who is married to your daughter whether you like it or not. CJ is part of my family now. Treat her with the respect she deserves. Or I *will* start interfering. I promise you that."

CHAPTER THREE

"How long has it been since we've seen Viv and Marja?" Alex asked as she pulled the car into the parking lot of the Park Restaurant.

"I don't remember." CJ was staring out the window.

Alex got out and locked the car after CJ exited.

"Think it's going to rain later?" Alex ventured.

CJ shrugged. "We're talking about the weather now? You know we have the same forecast in Denver every day from June to September. Warm with a chance of afternoon showers."

Alex stopped her on the sidewalk before they reached the front door.

"CJ," she said gently. "Let me go in and tell them we'll reschedule. You're not in a good place for a couple hours worth of Vivien's conversation. You didn't say three words to me all the way here."

CJ sighed.

"Alex, it took me three weeks to find a day all four of us could be in the same place at the same time," she said. "Viv and I have had to cancel our last two mani-pedi appointments, either her job or mine. Marja is on call every other weekend, and God knows you work about sixty hours a week, so could we just go in and have a nice time?"

Alex doubted a good time was in the offing. CJ sounded close to petulant. She said mildly, "Of course, sweetheart. Whatever you want. I just thought you might want to do this another time. It was a bit of a shock this morning. Maybe you should give yourself time to process a little bit."

"I don't want to *process* anything, Alex. I want to have lunch, okay?"

Alex opened the door.

The Park Restaurant had a bar filled with high-top tables on one side, full of old wood and young couples having Bloody Marys with their omelets or salads. The other side was a small and comfortable restaurant, booths with curved and padded benches in a deep green upholstery. The walnut wood paneling served as the perfect frame for the Park's displays of artwork for sale. The displays changed monthly and the effect differed depending on the genre of that month's artist. Last time they'd been here, Alex recalled, each painting featured a single piece of fruit rendered in vivid jewel tones unrelated to the actual fruit color—she remembered a bright purple apple with silver leaves. This month's painter favored graphic pieces in primary colors. Above the booth where Vivien sat waving to them hung an acrylic painting featuring a shield shape in bright yellow against a cobalt background. Alex thought it looked like an emblem for a classic comic book superhero.

Vivien Wong sprang out of the booth for hugs, CJ first and one for Alex too. She and Alex hadn't been particularly close in the beginning of her relationship with CJ, but time and a long, bitter separation when CJ had been gone for nine months the year before had drawn Alex into a warmer relationship with CJ's longtime friend.

Vivien's girlfriend Marja Erickson slid out of the booth behind Viv and waited her turn for hugs. Every time Alex saw them together, she tried to imagine how two women could look less alike. Marja looked like a power forward for a women's basketball team, her blond braid swinging casually over her polo shirt and jeans. Viv was petite and wore her gleaming black hair in what Alex supposed was still called a pixie cut. For a casual Saturday lunch, Vivien was wearing a gray pencil skirt and white silk blouse.

They arranged themselves in the booth, Viv and CJ sliding in to sit together with Alex and Marja across from each other at the semicircular table.

"Christ on toast, you took long enough to get here," Viv began. "We are starving. Somebody made me miss dinner last night!"

She gave a sly sideways glance at Marja, who smiled gently. For all her size, Alex had never seen her do anything that wasn't slow and deliberate.

"Not my fault," Marja said. "Something went wrong with a closing at work. She didn't get home until after eight and almost fell asleep in the bubble bath."

Vivien elbowed her. "Hey, don't give all our secrets away! They're going to think we're not having hot, sweaty sex on the couch every day as soon as I get home from work."

Alex opened the menu. "I could have done without the visual, Vivien, but thanks."

"Really, Viv," Marja murmured. "That happened, like, only two or three times."

Alex and Vivien laughed. CJ managed only a smile.

Vivien quickly turned to her. "Okay, what's wrong?"

"Not a thing," CJ said. "You're trying to talk about sex in public and Marja is shutting you down. Everything is exactly as usual."

Viv threw a questioning glance at Alex, who said, "If you're starving, let's order, okay? We can talk while someone is making us food."

As she was opening her mouth to pursue the question of why CJ wasn't acting normally, Marja asked softly, "What're you having, honey?"

"Hmph," Vivien said, conceding with poor grace for the moment. "What am I having? Something with hollandaise. A Benedict thingy. Because what's the point of brunch if you can't have a cream sauce?"

CJ said dryly, "That would depend on whether your doctor told you at your last appointment to lose twenty pounds."

"Is that what's gotten you so Miss Cranky Face?" Vivien asked her. "Well, screw the doctor. As long as Alex likes the way you look, who cares?" She turned to lift an eyebrow at Alex. "You're not unhappy, are you?"

Marja said, "This is none of our business, Viv."

"Oh, come on. You're not pressuring her, are you, Alex?" Vivien persisted.

"Of course not," Alex responded. "I love how CJ looks in every way. I just want her to be happy with herself. And healthy, because I'm planning on living with her for a very long time."

Vivien nodded approvingly. "Good answer."

CJ said, "I'm right here, y'all. You could talk to me instead of about me."

Alex winced a little. "Sorry, sweetheart, I just…"

The waiter appeared, pencil in hand. "Are we ready to order?"

They sorted out the food: crab benedict for Vivien, corned beef hash with poached eggs for Marja, with CJ choosing Eggs Santa Fe, a spicier dish with salsa. Alex decided on a spinach omelet. Vivien ordered a Bellini while the others settled for iced tea.

Before Vivien could resume her line of questioning, Marja said, "So I wonder if you two would be willing to talk shop for a couple of minutes."

Alex glanced at CJ before answering. "Sure. What's going on?"

"You know I've been running an evening group for adolescent girls," Marja began. "It's for kids in foster care, not old enough to go to emancipation classes yet, but starting to face adult issues. Foster parents do as good a job as they can, but they're usually swamped. And it's hard for them in public school. Kids in foster care get bullied sometimes and they never seem to have enough support or the right clothes." She smiled shyly. "You know how important clothes are to teenagers."

Viv and CJ nodded sympathetically. Alex drank her iced tea in silence. By the time she was a teenager, she was taking care of her younger sister Nicole while her father worked as a police officer. She never had time to think about anything else other than her coursework and tennis, which she had hoped would be her ticket to a college scholarship.

Life never worked out the way you thought it would, she mused. She was going to go to college, maybe become a teacher or a lawyer. She got the scholarship and a year later someone they'd never found ran down her father on a rainy night while he was working a traffic accident. At nineteen she had to quit college to take care of Nic, who was just entering high school. Alex joined the police force and had been there ever since.

She watched CJ, who was listening to Marja talk about her group. It was CJ who had urged Alex to finish her long-abandoned college degree. And it was falling in love with CJ that had been the proof of her long-suppressed suspicion that she was gay. Everything was different now.

"...so what do you think?" Marja was finishing up, and Alex realized that she'd missed the point of the conversation.

She caught CJ's look: a touch of recrimination and more than a bit of amusement. CJ said smoothly, "I think it's a great idea. My experience has been that the best way to overcome prejudice of any kind is to expose people to whatever it is they're biased against. The reality rarely matches their bigotry. Don't you agree, Alex?"

CJ's green eyes were twinkling at her. She knew Alex had no idea what the subject matter had been. Yet despite the fact that she was the butt of the joke, Alex was glad to see CJ's sense of humor returning.

"Yes," Alex replied. "Prejudice is the son of ignorance."

Marja looked at her in surprise and Vivien laughed. "What is that, the quote of the day?"

"No, that's me covering the fact that I zoned out and have no idea what we're talking about," Alex admitted.

Marja grinned and said, "Don't worry. I'm used to talking and people not listening. Occupational hazard for social workers."

Vivien said archly, "You're not talking about *me* not listening to you, I trust?"

"Oh, no, honey. I know you hang on my every word."

"So what is the topic?" Alex asked.

Marja said, "Most of these girls are pretty embittered about the system. I thought if they saw the police doing something for them, with them, it might give them a different perspective."

Alex was still lost, but CJ added, "We're thinking about a fundraiser, sponsored by the Colfax PD, where we work with the girls on some project to help support a scholarship fund."

"Oh. Got it. Great idea. What kind of fundraiser?"

"To be decided," Marja said. "But if you're willing to go to your boss about it, I'll get the agency to buy in."

They kicked around ideas for the fundraising project. Vivien's suggestion of a fashion show won the prize as least likely to succeed. By the time the food arrived, CJ seemed more herself and Alex was glad that they hadn't canceled. This was just what CJ needed, she thought, the distraction of her best friend.

As usual, Vivien dominated the conversation. They covered dogs (Marja wanted one and Vivien was trying to decide if she could put up with an animal), current events (a recent earthquake near San Francisco, Vivien's hometown) and the weather (summer was lingering longer than usual in Colorado).

While the plates were cleared, Marja said shyly, "Um, Alex? Vivien told me you used to play tennis."

"Yes. When I was a lot younger. Why?"

"I used to play back home. I was on the tennis team at high school, not that that meant much. I think there were only six girls in the whole place that played tennis."

"The joy of growing up in a small town," Vivien muttered.

Alex smiled. "It's been a while since I've played much. Sometimes CJ will go out with me and we'll play a set."

Marja turned to look at CJ. "You play too?"

"Don't look so surprised." CJ laughed a little. "My parents were very much into the country club social scene when I was growing up. Tennis lessons were *de rigueur*. Sorry," she added, seeing the confused look on Marja's face. "I just meant every properly brought up Southern girl took tennis lessons."

"Cool," Marja said. "I thought maybe, if you wanted to, we could all go out and play sometime. If you don't mind playing with somebody who just knocked the ball around at the local public park."

"Hey," Alex said quietly. "Me too. No country clubs here."

CJ said, "The tennis court's the same size for everybody, no matter where it is. I think this is a great idea! Think you can find your racket, Viv?"

"Ha, ha. I haven't set foot on a tennis court since I graduated from high school and got to leave my parents' influence. I'll have to buy a new one." She brightened at the thought. "And new shoes and a cute tennis dress and…hmm, they don't wear headbands anymore. Maybe a nice visor."

"Leave it to Viv to make playing tennis into an exercise in retail therapy," CJ said.

"Oh, don't be difficult. It'll be fun. We'll get something matchy-matchy."

"You'll have to play with Alex," CJ said. "If you and I play together, the two of them will kill us. I have trouble taking more than two or three games a set from Alex."

"What?" Vivien exclaimed. "You and Marja together are, like, twelve feet of tennis player. How are Alex and I going to compete?"

"Oh, come on, Vivien," Alex said. "Size doesn't matter, right?"

CJ joined in the general laughter and Alex relaxed. It looked like they were going to get through lunch successfully and Alex would be going home with a cheerful CJ instead of a grumpy one.

But then the check arrived. As usual, Vivien handed Marja her card to put in the credit card wallet. CJ dug her American

Express gold card out and said, "It's our turn, I think."

"I've got it," Vivien said. Alex had to acknowledge that Vivien was usually generous in matters financial. She made a lot more money in mortgage banking than a social worker and a couple of cops, so she deemed it her obligation to pick up the checks regularly.

CJ retorted irritably, "We don't need for you to pay every time, Vivien. We're not living in poverty, you know."

Vivien frowned at her. "Well, Christ in a three-piece suit, I know that. I just like to pay my way, that's all. Even if you do come from all that genteel Southern money."

CJ threw her napkin down. "I don't see why my grandfather's real estate investments are somehow more respectable than your parents making money in tech stocks," she snapped.

Alex reached over and said, "CJ, she didn't mean anything."

CJ turned on her. "I don't need for you to translate what people mean for me. I do that for a living, you know!"

There was a moment of stunned silence. Marja was looking worriedly from Vivien to CJ to Alex. Vivien was staring at CJ in disbelief.

Finally Vivien said, "Okay. What the holy fucking hell is the matter with you?"

"Nothing." CJ sat back sullenly. "You were being an ass."

"I'm always an ass," Vivien replied, shrugging. "You're used to it. You're supposed to laugh at me or ignore me. Now, what the hell is going on?"

CJ said nothing.

Marja said, "Stop it, Viv. Leave her alone. Everybody's entitled to an off day."

"Oh, don't go all social worker on me. Are you going to talk to me or not, CJ?"

At last CJ unfolded her arms.

"Sorry, Viv. Let's forget it, all right?"

Alex said softly, "Sweetheart. Tell her, please."

CJ released a deep sigh. She began to toy with a knife left on the table, turning the silver handle over between her fingers.

"We had a visit at the condo this morning. From my mother."

"Your…for a minute there, I thought you said your *mother*," Vivien exclaimed.

Alex said, "In person, unannounced and unexpected."

It was one of the few occasions that Alex had actually seen Vivien's jaw drop.

Marja said quietly, "Sorry, I don't understand."

Alex opened her mouth to explain, but CJ cut her off.

"Why would you? Y'all haven't heard the story of my dear mama and her only daughter. She threw me out of the house when I told her I was a lesbian and I haven't spoken to her in almost fourteen years."

"Oh." Marja managed to convey compassion and surprise into a single syllable.

Vivien found her voice at last. "Are you fucking kidding me?" she bellowed. "Seriously? I hope you threw her out of *your* house on her ass!"

Several diners at nearby tables glanced their way, in curiosity or worry.

"Viv," Marja murmured.

"Well, honestly!" Vivien said, managing to slightly lower her tone. "What the fuck did she think she was doing? Trying to make up after all this time?"

CJ gave a bitter little laugh. "Hardly. Apparently she actually stationed her limo driver outside the condo to try to keep Alex from even coming in."

"Oh, I'll bet that went over really well," Vivien said. "How long did it take you to get past him, Alex?"

"About thirty seconds," Alex acknowledged. "She was not happy to include me in the conversation."

"No shit. So what the hell did she want, CJ?"

CJ moved on to playing with an unused spoon, turning it over and back again and again.

Alex waited. It wasn't her story to tell.

Finally CJ said, "My brother's in trouble. She wants me to come home to Savannah to help him."

"And you told her to go fuck herself, I hope," Vivien snapped.

"I haven't told her anything."

"What the…" Vivien began, but Marja cut her off.

"Okay, enough, Viv," she said. "Anything we can do to help, CJ?"

Alex threw her a grateful look. CJ shook her head.

"No. I just need some time. And I'm sorry I snapped your head off, Viv. This has really thrown me. I've thought about how I might react if I ever saw her again. But this was nothing like what I thought about or expected. I just need to sort out how I feel."

Vivien reached over and wrapped her elegant fingers around CJ's forearm.

"You know how I feel about this," she said. "But I'm here for you, kiddo. We all are, right? So you take your time. I'm sure you'll make the right decision."

Alex wondered if CJ would even know what the right decision might be.

CHAPTER FOUR

The warm weather continued on Sunday. After brunch CJ announced that her balcony herb garden needed tending. She put on sunscreen, hat and gardening gloves and went out onto the balcony. She closed the French door behind her.

Alex knew that the gardening was therapeutic, and she was happy to see CJ taking the time she needed. She put their plates in the dishwasher, scrubbed the pan and went into her office to work.

After a while she heard CJ come in and then heard the sound of water running as CJ washed up. When CJ didn't appear in their office Alex stayed there, finishing up her report reading and preparing notes for her usual Monday morning meeting. Once a week she met with the entire detective staff for a rundown of current cases and any other news she needed to share. She tolerated the constant stream of memos, emails and notices that were an inevitable adjunct to police work pretty well. But she preferred talking with her detectives, reading their expressions, exchanging ideas. Being on a team was her favorite part of police work and she liked being a leader, helping her cops catch the bad guys.

It had taken her some time living with CJ for Alex to let go of being in charge at home. CJ liked to talk out problems and she used information to make decisions based on her instincts. When she shut a conversation down, it meant that her feelings were in conflict.

Alex printed out the notes for tomorrow and went to find her partner.

CJ was on the couch with her long legs stretched out. She'd changed into a disreputable pair of jeans with holes in both knees and a shirt that had "Colfax PD" printed on it. A new biography of Emily Dickinson was in her hands.

"Hey," she said as Alex came in. "Finish working?"

"Well, for today. How's the book?"

"Interesting. One of the author's theories is that Emily was either a lesbian or bisexual."

"I had no idea. How do they know? Were there gay bars in Amherst?"

"In the nineteenth century that seems unlikely. How about a drink?"

Alex was surprised but said, "Okay. It's five o'clock somewhere."

CJ sat up. "Actually, it's five o'clock in Savannah."

Alex stopped. "Are we talking about this now?"

"Drink first." CJ started to get up.

"I'll get it," Alex offered. "Chardonnay?"

She put on some music, then settled on the couch next to CJ, handing her a glass. They sipped and listened to Tony Bennett for a while.

At length CJ said, "I'm sorry. I've been a real bitch this weekend."

"Kinda. Not really bitchy so much as grumpy."

"Well, I was certainly bitchy on the phone with my mother."

"Ah. And how did that go?"

"Not particularly well. She seems fixated on the fact that I somehow owe her or Clayton or maybe generations of ancestors long dead some kind of obligation to clear the family name."

"I don't suppose she mentioned the part where she threw you out of the family."

"She won't discuss it."

"Is she acting like it never happened?"

CJ took a drink and set her glass down on the table with a clink. "Apropos of nothing, don't you think it's silly we call these coffee tables? I hardly ever set my coffee cup on it. I usually set it down on the breakfast bar. Or the bathroom vanity while I'm getting ready in the morning."

Alex said, "Next time you try to change the subject maybe you could be a little less obvious about it. And as for the table, we could start calling it the wine table."

CJ laughed a little and abruptly leaned into her. With her mouth an inch from Alex's lips she whispered, "Do you know what I love about you?"

"Tell me," Alex said softly.

"Everything." CJ kissed her.

After a couple of minutes, Alex muttered, "This is a lot better way to change the subject, but shouldn't we get back to talking about your mother?"

CJ sighed. "If we must. Where were we?"

"You were explaining how your mother could conveniently forget that she tossed you out of the family."

"Oh, it's worse than that. She has managed to make it my fault that I had to leave home. Somehow because of that I'm now responsible for saving the honor of the St. Clair name."

"You're kidding."

CJ shook her head. "Not really. Don't discount the importance of family for Southerners. For all of her holier-than-thou attitude, Mama is really scared."

"This sounds to me like maybe you've made a decision."

CJ picked up her wineglass again.

"Oh, darlin', I don't know what to do. Do I really owe my family something in spite of everything? Do I give up my self-respect by running home just because my mother asked me? I've been over this and over it again and I just don't know."

Alex rubbed her back lightly.

"You don't have to decide right this minute," Alex said softly.

"No," CJ admitted reluctantly, "but she's not going to let up until I give her an answer. She's flying back tomorrow and she wants me to go back with her." CJ rolled her eyes. "What a horrifying thought. Three or four hours on an airplane with Mama. I'd rather have a root canal. Or two."

"So tell her no," Alex suggested.

CJ picked up her glass again and twirled the stem a bit. "I would but…I keep thinking about Clayton."

Alex was quiet for a moment, listening to Tony croon about his broken heart. "You're afraid he'll be convicted?"

CJ took a sip of the straw-colored wine. "If he is, I hope it's because he's guilty. I just keep worrying."

"That he did it."

"No. I'm worried that he didn't."

Alex leaned back in surprise. "Isn't that what we're hoping for?"

"You know as well as I do that the conviction rate in this country is over ninety percent. Even with a good private attorney, the odds are really stacked against him. If he killed Amy, I hope they throw him in prison and lock the door forever. But if he didn't…"

Alex said, "I know. But you need to think this through. What if you try to help him and they convict him anyway? What if you investigate and find out, God forbid, that he really did it? What if you help him get an acquittal and later find out that he was guilty after all? It's like a minefield."

CJ gave her a long look. "You've been giving this a little thought too, I see."

Alex took her hand and laced their fingers together. "Maybe."

"You don't think I should go, do you?"

"I didn't say that. All I want is for you to consider the implications of the choice you make. Because whatever happens, whatever you do or don't do, you need to be at peace with the decision."

CJ finished her wine.

"I'm damned if I do and damned if I don't. You're right, it's a minefield. And all the mines are filled with guilt."

Alex smiled a little. "Way to take a metaphor one step too far," she said. "What do you want to do now?"

"I have an overwhelming desire for Chinese food."

"Am I getting out the wok?"

"Nope," CJ said. "We're ordering delivery for an early dinner and you're going to find me a sappy movie to watch. I want to turn my brain off for a while."

Alex considered. "I'll find something appropriate for the mood today," she said. "How about *Terms of Endearment*? Or wait, even better: *Steel Magnolias*."

CJ smirked. "You think you're so funny, don't you? No mother-daughter relationships allowed. Now bring me the menu from Happy Dragon."

"Why," Alex complained, "do you eat all the pancakes when there's still moo shu pork left?"

"I like the pancakes better than the pork," CJ explained. "There are some tortillas in the kitchen that'll work."

"No, thanks." Alex folded the top of the white paper box back into place. "I'll save it and put the moo shu in your omelet in the morning."

"Eww. No, thank you. Any sweet and sour chicken left?"

Alex passed her the cardboard container and they split the rest of the food. They watched Kevin Kline and Meg Ryan get together on the airplane at the end of *French Kiss* and Alex cleaned up plates while the credits rolled. When she returned, CJ had already picked up her Dickinson book again.

"I'd like to read for a bit longer," CJ said. "If you're tired, it's okay to go on to bed."

"I hardly did anything today. And even I can stay up past seven o'clock. I also have half a Sue Grafton mystery left."

"Sue Grafton makes you happy."

They settled in on the couch in their usual positions: CJ had her legs propped up on the renamed wine table before her, Alex lying with her feet crossed on CJ's thigh. After a while, CJ used her free hand to stroke Alex gently from the ankles up.

From deep within Alex could feel herself relax. This was her favorite moment in the week, alone with CJ in the quiet.

After a while, CJ got up and made tea, bringing the mugs back. Alex smiled her thanks and they read some more. Usually Alex was earlier to bed by an hour or two, but tonight CJ was the first to close her book.

"Tired?" Alex asked.

"Not really," CJ admitted. "But I really think I need a shower before bed. I hate getting in between clean sheets with sunscreen on."

Alex looked into the smoky green eyes and saw what she was expecting to see. A pleasant warmth began to uncoil low in her body as she watched CJ cross the room, pulling off her T-shirt as she went.

She dropped it on the floor of the living room and looked back over her shoulder at Alex.

"You're so untidy," Alex said, smiling.

"You may have mentioned that before," CJ replied.

Alex watched as CJ removed her bra, her back modestly turned. She lifted the bra by one strap and let it fall near the T-shirt.

"You're trying to seduce me, Mrs. Robinson," Alex said. "Aren't you?"

CJ turned the corner into the hall. A moment later her jeans flew into the doorway. Alex waited and a moment later CJ's black underwear followed.

Alex loved a good mystery novel, but Sue Grafton in print was no competition for CJ in the flesh. She put the book on the table.

Alex retrieved CJ's shirt from its resting place and collected the ripped jeans, bra and finally CJ's underwear from the floor. She tossed all the clothes along with her own clothing into the hamper.

When Alex opened the shower door, CJ was facing away from her, finishing the last rinse of her hair. Alex stepped in behind her. The water was warm on her chest, the tile like ice under her fingers.

She brought her hands to CJ's shoulders, then ran them lightly down her wet back. She felt her shudder and begin to turn around.

"No," Alex said. "Stay there."

She pushed CJ gently forward into the shower wall. The steaming water sluiced between them. Alex pressed closer, wrapping her arms around her to caress her breasts. Her own body felt taut and she rubbed herself against CJ, sliding herself up and down against her skin.

CJ gasped and reached back, searching for Alex.

Alex grasped CJ's wrists and pushed them against the wall before her. "Leave them here."

Another noise came from CJ's throat, a groan that filled Alex with pleasure. She continued the full body caresses.

Steaming water, the cold tile and the smooth silk of CJ's skin under her hands heightened all of Alex's senses. She loved the curves and flare of CJ's backside and the more she touched her lover the louder she became. Finally CJ pushed herself back into Alex as she slid her hands down the shower wall, stepping her legs apart in blatant invitation.

Alex kissed down her back, then slipped her hand in between supple, inviting flesh.

CJ groaned, "That's so good."

As Alex entered her, CJ clenched and twisted. Alex held her in place gently and murmured, "Come on, baby. Come on."

She reached all the deepest places within CJ, the way she knew she wanted to be touched, stroked, caressed.

Alex knew every noise CJ could make, every movement of her hips, every desperate clench as she neared her orgasm. She waited for the shuddering to begin, then went deeper.

At her climax, CJ clenched her hands and cried out incoherently one last time. Alex wondered if there was a more satisfying feeling in the world than this moment of giving pleasure, seeing CJ buckle beneath her hands, knowing she alone could bestow this gift to the woman she loved.

She couldn't imagine anything better.

Alex was almost asleep with CJ curled comfortably behind her, warm and pliable.

CJ murmured, "I have to go."

"Home, you mean?"

"Home is here with you, darlin'. But to Savannah, yes. I'll figure out how to try to wrap up a couple of things at work and see what time off I can manage."

"Okay," Alex said. What else could she say? "Any idea how long you'll be gone?"

"It's hard to guess, but ten days maybe. Two weeks, tops. If I haven't found anything helpful by then I probably won't."

"Okay," Alex said again.

CJ squeezed Alex's hand. "Aren't you going to ask me why I'm going?"

"I think I already know, but tell me."

Alex felt the soft exhale of breath against her cheek.

"Because no matter what I find out or don't find out, I'll know that I tried. If I don't go, I'll always wonder if I could have helped. It's not for my mother. It's not even for Clayton. I'm going for myself. Whatever happens, I'm coming home to you and it will be all right."

Alex felt her shoulders relax.

"Yes," she whispered. "It will be all right. Do what you need to do. I'll be right here."

CHAPTER FIVE

"May I get you a drink?"

CJ looked up at the flight attendant. She'd just settled in to her first-class seat. People flying economy were piling into the plane behind her, so they were at least ten minutes from takeoff.

"Yes, thanks," CJ said. "Ginger ale, please." It was still morning and
she had work to do on this flight.

Once they were safely in the air, CJ dug out her tablet from the pocket in front of her. Yesterday she had gotten the police files from her brother's attorney via email. CJ transferred the files into her tablet, pleased that she didn't have to juggle paper files on the plane.

She glanced at the heavyset man in the seat beside her. She imagined that he wouldn't have appreciated glancing over as she looked at crime scene photos or a coroner's report.

Miller Ross, her brother's defense attorney, had done a thorough job of discovery. Idly CJ wondered how much he charged Clayton—or more likely her mother—for the time it had taken to go through all this.

A murder investigation generated a massive amount of paperwork. In addition to all the crime scene information, there were lab reports and dozens of witness statements. CJ knew she wouldn't get through all of them on the flight, but she hoped to read through the main documents before she landed.

She spent a few moments sorting the documents into folders. Evidence files and search warrants into one, medical and lab reports into another, police reports into a third. Organizing the files helped organize her thoughts. At some point she'd want to read every word, but now she mentally listed her priorities. Initial reports and crime scene first, the way she'd have done it if she were investigating the case herself.

On her last evening, Amy had attended an MS support group meeting at a local Lutheran church. The group hadn't broken up until after eight, so it was getting dark. She asked a friend to walk with her out to their cars in the church parking lot.

According to the friend's statement, they were near Amy's car when a man appeared in front of them. He demanded Amy's purse, then apparently shot her for no reason.

CJ steeled herself to look at the crime scene photo of Amy's body. She had seen her share of corpses but seeing someone you'd known in life was different. Amy was on her back, a little blood on her chest. Most of the bleeding had been internal. Her ankles were crossed in the classic "deadman's cross," the sure sign of a victim shot while standing.

Her eyes were open in the photo taken at the scene. She must have died right away, with no time even to close them.

Amy hadn't resisted or so the witness said. CJ made a note of her name—Linn Childs—and her address. She'd be one of her first interviews.

Assuming she was willing to talk to CJ at all. She and Alex had discussed the challenge of investigating a crime without the authority of her badge. Alex reassured her.

"You're the best interviewer I know," Alex said. "Besides, you know these people. You grew up there. You'll figure out how to get what you need."

CJ stared out the window. Far below her, beneath the wispy clouds, lay the quilt of the Kansas farmland, chocolate brown and dark green and harvest gold in patches. She hoped Alex was right. Part of her felt like a reader picking up a novel she'd first read long ago. She wondered if the characters or settings would have changed so much she might not recognize them.

She paged through to the coroner's report, trying to emotionally distance herself from the memories of Amy. Amy had met Clayton at the University of Georgia and CJ had been a bridesmaid at the wedding. The Amy she recalled had been sweet and shy and pretty, her petite dark looks a nice contrast to Clayton's sandy hair and outgoing personality. She'd also been a devoted mother to their baby, Laura.

Don't think about the Amy you knew. For this case she has to be just the victim. Single gunshot to the chest, massive damage to the heart. Death would have come within a minute or two. *Nice shot. Lucky or a lot of practice?*

Almost without thinking CJ brushed her fingertips across the top of the scar just below the center of the top of her shirt. If the bullet had gone just few millimeters to the left, she would have been as dead as Amy.

She read through some of the follow-up reports and the evidence logs. Amy's purse was found in a trash can outside the church within a couple of hours after the shooting. Nothing missing from the purse. No fingerprints, which wasn't all that surprising. Usable prints were a lot rarer than most people thought.

CJ finished her drink and asked for coffee with lunch. As she ate she knew she would have drawn the same conclusions as the lead detective on the case, a Sergeant Monroe. Taking Amy's purse had been a pretext for the murder. So what was the motive?

Barring insanity, motive for murder usually came down to one of three things: money, sex or revenge. She'd heard other detectives say that love was a motive, but CJ knew better. Love, real love couldn't lead to evil. But love could twist so quickly into hatred, mutating in a whisper. CJ had experienced it herself in the tritest of circumstances: she'd walked in on her first girlfriend in bed with another woman. It was the ugliest moment of emotion she could remember experiencing. If she'd had a gun in her hand, might she have used it in that moment?

This murder seemed almost impersonal. The killer hadn't waited for an opportunity to stab, to strangle, to bludgeon. One clean shot and Amy was dead. It certainly looked like money was the likely reason.

The attendant cleared her tray and CJ returned to her reading. The police had contacted Clayton late that evening. Amy's parents were dead and CJ supposed that he was the closest they could find to be next of kin. Other than Laura, of course, but no fifteen-year-old girl would be the first to be told about her mother's death if the police could help it. Clayton talked to the investigators voluntarily and agreed to a gunshot residue test on his hands. CJ went into another file to locate the GSR test result: it was negative.

Which didn't mean much. Gloves would have taken care of that. She went back to the information provided by Linn Childs, but there was no mention of gloves in the initial report.

CJ frowned. It was a minor detail, but it bothered her. She made a note to follow up. Her curiosity aroused, she also looked for any gun residue test results on the hoodie, but those were negative as well.

That was unusual. She would have expected at least trace amounts.

She scanned many of the supplemental reports. The detectives figured out that Clayton had an insurance policy on Amy, and that, along with the information that Clayton's finances were precarious, spelled out a convincing motive.

Apparently they'd had enough to convince a judge to issue a search warrant. A week or so after the shooting, the police executed the warrant for Clayton's house and car. A hooded jacket similar to the one worn by the shooter had turned up in Clayton's closet and hidden in the trunk of his car the cops found a nine millimeter semiautomatic.

She went back again to the lab reports. Ballistics confirmed that the gun in Clayton's car was the murder weapon. The weapon itself had been reported stolen several months ago by the owner. It could have been bought and sold illegally several times since then, which made it essentially untraceable.

There was no trace evidence on the jacket except for a single hair, which was found to be "microscopically similar" to Clayton's.

Where had Clayton been that night? She found the supplemental witness statement and saw that he had lawyered up by then. He was home alone, he said. Laura was staying over with a friend that night.

CJ didn't have to make a note to talk to her niece. She was simultaneously looking forward to and dreading the conversation. God alone knew what Clayton had told his daughter about the wicked sinner of the family.

After glancing through the rest of the files, CJ found nothing else of much significance. There were interviews with Clayton's newest ex-wife, Missy, his current girlfriend, even his partner and the employees at his dental practice. She made notes, preparing a rough plan of which people to interview.

She closed the tablet and sat back. It was a circumstantial case, but a solid one. The eyewitness hadn't been able to identify Clayton as the shooter, but with a motive, without an alibi and with the gun and jacket tying him to the crime, it looked like a good case. CJ had seen people convicted on less evidence.

As far as CJ could tell, Clayton had insisted on his innocence from the first interview to his arrest. In CJ's experience, most criminals confessed eventually but not all. It was a small point in her brother's favor.

I'll know when I talk to him. I'll be able to tell.

I hope.

Savannah was already more than forty years old when shots were fired at Lexington and Concord. General James Oglethorpe arrived in 1733, carrying his comprehensive town plan with him. The downtown district still demonstrated his passion for the Enlightenment, green parks carefully distributed within a tidy grid.

CJ realized she'd forgotten how green her city was. Grass in Colorado was green only through diligent use of water and fertilizer, but here everything was lush and still blooming.

She wished she could take a walk in Forsyth Park along the trails, maybe sit near the huge fountain at the north end. She remembered going once as a child to watch them dye the water green for St. Patrick's Day.

Sighing, she turned the silver rental car north toward downtown. The Oglethorpe building was close to the Chatham County Courthouse and shared its traditional red brick architecture with a white-columned front. It looked old but well-kept, like a Southern gentleman's meticulously groomed white mustache. CJ was pleased to see people coming in and out of the building, a sign that it was full of tenants and thriving. It still felt odd to her that she owned the building. Well, technically her trust owned it, but as the only beneficiary, she felt a strong proprietary interest in the property.

She didn't know the receptionist at the front desk but the woman obviously knew who she was dealing with, giving CJ a bright smile and permission to go directly into Roger Thornton's office.

He was waiting for her, a broad smile showing every crease in his long, drooping face. He rose slowly from behind his desk, using his knotted, blue-veined hands to help himself up.

"Oh my dear Belle!" he exclaimed. "I am so happy to see you!"

Impulsively CJ dropped her purse on the desk and went around to go into his arms. The flood of joy surprised her. Roger had been her grandfather's law partner and oldest friend and hugging him was like connecting with her family again.

He patted her back, then released her to look at her with interest.

"You look wonderful, my dear child."

CJ laughed a little. "Older. Not quite a slip of a girl anymore," she answered.

He gave a deep rumbling chuckle in response. "Well, as your grandfather used to say, it's either get older or die."

"He was a wise man."

"Let's sit down," he suggested. "No, you sit over here on the couch."

The couch looked comfortable with its broad leather cushions, but CJ wondered if, once down, Roger would be able to get up again.

He chuckled again at her look.

"Don't worry. I know my limitations. The straight chair for me."

Before he joined her, he pressed a button on his desk.

"I thought we'd finish our business first," he said. "Just some signatures and the latest statement. I wondered if you wanted to go over anything in it in person."

"I doubt it," CJ said. "If I have a question, y'all have answered it right away. Tell me about Abby and the family."

They chatted about Roger's daughters, grandchildren and his championship bulldogs. The inner door to his office opened and two people entered: a young man carrying a tea tray and a slender woman wearing a beautifully cut lavender suit. She had a slim file folder in one elegant hand.

Roger began the struggle to rise from his chair, but she laid her free hand lightly on his shoulder.

"Don't get up." She turned to smile at CJ and said, "The perfect gentleman, as always."

CJ returned the smile. "He always has been," she responded. "I'm CJ St. Clair."

"Gina Waters," she replied, offering a hand to shake.

"Have we met?" CJ cocked her head slightly. "You look a little familiar."

Roger said, "She should. Remember Betty?"

"Betty! Of course! My goodness, how long was she your admin assistant?"

"Only twenty-four years," Roger chuckled. "Regina was a little girl when Betty started."

Gina laughed. "It was a little like growing up in the firm."

The young man set down the tray on the table between them while Gina seated herself.

"Thank you, David," Roger said, and the young man left, closing the door softly behind him. CJ smiled to herself, noting happily that the woman with dark skin was staying for the meeting while the man with light skin was just there to deliver the snacks.

Gina poured cups for the three of them and sat back, waiting for Roger to start the discussion.

He began. "Gina has been with us since she graduated from law school. I've been very impressed with her work in the estate planning side of the practice and she's recently been elevated to partner, I'm happy to report. I've been letting her work on your trust quite a bit, and I wanted you to meet her, Belle."

Gina flashed her a quick look. CJ said, "Belle was the name I used growing up. You might call it my nom de home."

Gina had a nice laugh, her teeth white and perfect against her skin.

"I like that. My given name is Regina. I suppose that's my nom de home. My mother still calls me that."

"Is she well?"

"A bit of arthritis, but she gets around pretty well. Church suppers, knitting club, volunteer work—I would find her schedule exhausting."

"It's her chance to do what she wants," Roger said. "She should enjoy it."

CJ gave him an appraising look. "Is that what's happening here, Roger? Are you finally going to retire?"

He replaced his teacup into the saucer with a clatter and set it on the table.

"Not exactly," he answered. "But most days I'm satisfied strolling in and reading the *ABA Journal* and going to lunch. Not much practice of law there. Gina is twice as good as I am."

"Roger," Gina murmured.

"Well, you will be soon. And I want our best client to have the best lawyer. So, what do you think, Belle? There are a couple of other young bucks, but I think Gina is your choice."

CJ leaned forward and grasped his hand.

"On one condition."

"What would that be, my dear?"

"I can still call you and talk Georgia football."

His laugh was a deep rumble that started in his chest and journeyed upward.

"Of course! Of course! Football talk is always welcome."

Gina said, "I know I'm not Roger, but I can assure you, Ms. St. Clair, you will get the same attention and service you're used to receiving from us." She handed over a card, adding, "This is my private line. You can call me anytime with any question. Though I'm not as proficient as Roger at dissecting a zone defense."

CJ said, "I'll be in town for a while. Perhaps we can have lunch or something."

"I'd like that."

"Good. And it's CJ from here on, all right?"

They finished the paperwork quickly and Gina excused herself. When she was gone, Roger asked, "So are you all right with this, really?"

"I'm sure she'll be great. If you trust her, that's good enough for me."

She poured him more tea. He accepted the cup and said, "You want to talk about Clayton."

It wasn't a question. CJ sank back into the glove-soft leather of the couch. She could hear the ticktock of the old-fashioned carriage clock on his desk. The rest of the sounds around them were muffled by the thick beige carpet and burgundy drapes framing the windows. It was good to see Roger again, the last and best connection she had with her grandfather, but no part of her was looking forward to this conversation.

"Yes," she said at last. "I don't know him. I haven't seen him in almost fifteen years. I know it sounds terrible, but as an adult I really don't understand anything about him."

Roger's faded blue eyes were almost hidden by his drooping eyelids, but she could see the faraway expression.

"When you reach my age," he began, "you realize most people's stories are really very simple. Human needs don't vary that much, although the methods we use to get them met are infinite in their diversity. Some of us are better at finding happiness than others. Or perhaps we're just more persistent, or perhaps it's all some great plan we can't see." He returned from where he'd been and smiled at her indulgently.

"For a long time, my dear, I thought you were going to struggle with your life. You had moments of unhappiness growing up I didn't understand from far away. I think perhaps your grandfather knew, which is why he provided for you in his will. In the event, when you told me what had happened with your mother, I understood much more clearly." He shook his head.

"You were brave enough to leave, Belle, and seek your own chance at the life you wanted. And perhaps against all odds, you have succeeded. You seem happy."

CJ thought of Alex and said, "I'm very happy, Roger."

He nodded. "When she came to see me last year your…Ms. Ryan seemed very determined to get you back. So I'm pleased that you found what you seemed to want the most: someone to love who was worthy of your affection."

CJ blinked hard against the sudden surge of emotion. There had been times when the possibility of joy seemed impossible. Would she live through those times again for the life she had now?

In a heartbeat.

"Is that what you're telling me about Clayton?" she asked. "He's searching for happiness?"

"Certainly. But in my opinion, Clayton has made an error in judgment that many people, both women and men, often make."

"Which is?"

"He has mistaken the process of falling in love for a permanent condition. He wasn't willing to put in the work to turn his relationships into a lifetime commitment." He smiled and the deep creases seemed to swallow his face again. "I speak, of course, from the perspective of a man who has awakened next to the same woman for the last fifty-two years."

"And no fighting in all that time, I'm sure," CJ said, teasing him.

"All couples fight." He shook a gnarled finger at her. "If you stop fighting, you stop caring and then your relationship is doomed."

"I'll remember that the next time Alex and I have a disagreement. So what are you saying about Clayton? That he's a romantic?"

"An immature one. Although lately I may have seen some signs of him growing up a bit. He's had a lot of difficult lessons and some of them may be beginning to sink in."

CJ listened to the clock ticking for a few moments. Then she said, "I have to ask you this, Roger. Do you think he killed Amy?"

His head sank onto his chest, doubling his chins.

"Honestly? If they had been fighting about Laura or money and he struck out at her…perhaps he could. Perhaps we all could in the right circumstances. But like this, a deliberate ambush, planned and cold-blooded? No. I think not."

CJ exhaled in relief.

Roger lifted his head and smiled a little. "I'm fairly certain an old man's opinion isn't going to count for much with the jury."

"Maybe not. But it helps me. I'm meeting Clayton for lunch in forty-five minutes. After almost fifteen years, I hope I recognize him."

Josie's was a diner that looked as though it had been in the same location since before CJ was born. It clung unabashedly to a fifties' aesthetic from the black and white tile floor to the red vinyl booths. The tables were trimmed in shiny chrome and the photo of Elvis in mid hip swivel adorned the booth where CJ waited facing the door.

She sipped at her iced tea and winced. She'd forgotten when she ordered it that sweet tea was the norm here and she'd long ago gotten accustomed to the Western version served without sugar. *Funny how quickly your tastes could change.*

They were busy at the lunch hour, but the waitresses were efficient, never making a trip to or from the kitchen without carrying food or busing tables. Food service was hard work. CJ remembered.

She squeezed more lemon into her tea to cut the syrupy flavor. The meeting with her mother had gone so badly that she was dreading the next hour with her brother. They had never been close as siblings, too different in their tastes and interests. And the underlying current between them was competition. CJ could acknowledge that now. She had been much beloved by her father, and she sensed Clayton always was an afterthought. He'd tried everything: first tennis, then football, dating the well-connected society girls their mother approved of, going to the University of Georgia. Studying dentistry had been a last-ditch effort to impress their parents, she suspected, but her mother had made it clear that that was a poor substitute for being a cardiac surgeon. She never knew whether her father was disappointed.

Was everyone's family a mystery? Children's perceptions of their parents necessarily changed with maturity, but maybe the dynamics were set early and never really changed. CJ had always known her father adored her and was equally sure her mother didn't like her. What had Clayton thought? She had no idea.

"Belle?"

She looked up. She'd missed him coming in.

CJ slid out of the booth, and they had an awkward moment of deciding whether or not to hug. After a moment Clayton reached over and squeezed her forearm gently.

"Hi," he said. "It's me."

In some ways he'd aged well. He was actually more trim than she remembered, his forty-year-old belly hardly pushing against his belt. She envied what must be his dedication to his diet or his workout routine.

But the years were visible in other ways. He was only an inch or two taller than her own five ten and that seemed shorter than she remembered. His sandy hair was lightening to a faded yellow-white and was thinning on top. At least he hadn't resorted to a comb-over.

He still had her daddy's eyes, blue and bright. There were frown lines set deep into his forehead and lining his mouth.

"Thanks for meeting me here," he said. "It's close to the office and the food is pretty good. Also it's cheap."

She looked at him again. Nice oxford cloth shirt, designer tie, gold Rolex. He didn't appear to be wallowing in poverty.

The waitress appeared and said, "Hi, Doc. What's for lunch today?"

He gave her a dazzling smile and leaned back against the red vinyl. "Well, you tell me, darlin'. What looks good back there?"

"Special is the chicken fried, but Ernie's being chintzy with the steak. You need to go meatloaf."

"I always take your advice, you know that. Meatloaf and double the mashed potatoes. And you save me a piece of that coconut cream pie, honey."

Well, apparently it wasn't his diet he was working on.

"And what about you, miss?"

"Chef's salad, ranch on the side please," CJ said, trying to feel virtuous instead of deprived.

Clayton waited until the waitress had left before he said, "I think you should know I didn't send Mama out to get you. In fact, I told her not to bother you."

"Why?" she asked.

He shrugged. "I think this whole thing is bullshit, that's why. I wasn't there. I didn't do it. I…" He stopped for a moment and his face became unreadable. After a minute he resumed, "I would never have hurt Amy."

CJ decided to prod him a bit.

"You were divorced. Presumably you weren't close pals."

He dug a well-manicured nail into a tiny chip in the Formica top.

"We were still raising a daughter together. We were…on good terms. I had no reason."

"The police think you did it for money, Mama said."

"The cops! They have no idea what they're talking about."

CJ watched him for a moment. Something seemed off, but she didn't know him well enough to know what it was. "I think I should tell you a few things, Clayton."

He looked surprised. "Okay," he said reluctantly.

"I am a cop. I joined the sheriff's office when I got to Colorado, and I've been in law enforcement since."

"So, what? You ride around in a car and give out tickets, like that?"

"I did, for a while. I've been an accident investigator, a detective, even gone undercover a few times. I'm currently in charge of Internal Affairs at a suburban police department. I'm a lieutenant."

"Good for you. What's your point, exactly?"

"I know a lot about how criminal investigations work. And I've read almost all of the police files in Amy's murder and it's my professional opinion that you are in trouble."

His face settled into the lines she'd noted earlier, nearly a scowl.

"You flew halfway across the country to tell me that?"

"No. I flew here to try to save your tail from spending the rest of your life in Reidsville."

The scowl deepened and she saw his skin flush a darker red.

"You're not exactly being tactful here, Belle."

"You don't have time for me to be tactful. I talked to your lawyer on the phone last week. He's an expert in his field as I'm an expert in mine and we agree. We need to find some reasonable doubt or you're going to prison."

He stared at her. "I don't believe it. I didn't do anything! How can I get convicted?"

The food arrived, but Clayton seemed too agitated to eat. He pushed his plate away a few inches and scrubbed a hand across his face.

CJ said, "I know I'm scaring you. That was my intent. I need for you take this as seriously as possible. I need your help."

He stared down at his meatloaf a moment, then pulled the plate back toward him. He picked up his fork and said, "Okay. All right. I get it. What do you need?"

First hurdle passed. CJ doctored her salad with dressing and mixed the diced meats and cheese into the lettuce.

"You need to realize that whoever killed Amy wanted the police to arrest you."

He stopped in midchew. "What?" he mumbled around his food.

"Think about it. He kills your ex-wife in front of a witness. He makes sure he can't be identified. It's a bad attempt at a robbery, making it clear that murder was the objective. The killer uses a hooded jacket, yours or one that looks like yours. He uses your gun, which he returns to your car."

He put the fork down again. At this rate it was going to take him three hours to eat lunch.

"Oh, hell," he said. "It's a frame-up, that's what you call it, right?"

"Yes. And here's the next question. Was the killer's real motive to kill Amy? Or was she merely a convenient victim to implicate you?"

"You're not…you're saying some bastard killed Amy because of me?" His face had changed from dark red to a sickly pale shade.

"We don't know that," CJ said quickly. "But it's a possibility we need to consider. I'll be doing some digging into Amy's life, but I need for you to tell me who might hate you enough to do this."

He stared at the twin white mounds of mashed potatoes, drowned in brown gravy. He shoveled in several forkfuls, and CJ ate her own lunch, giving him time to absorb the implications.

Clayton, like every dentist she'd ever known, had perfectly groomed nails. On the backs of his hands she could see the tiny sandy hairs springing up. During the long summers when they were children, his hair would lighten to almost white in the summer sun.

CJ had a sudden memory of her mother's voice ordering her inside, telling her ladies shouldn't be out in the sun.

Clayton put his fork down. "Someone who hates me enough to frame me for murder. Belle, goddammit, nobody hates me that much."

After a long drink of iced tea, CJ answered, "It's possible that someone wanted Amy dead and you were just a convenient suspect. But I'm not sure. How about your other ex-wives?"

He stared thoughtfully over her head. "I can't feature Paula caring enough one way or the other."

"You married her right after you divorced Amy, right?"

The scowl returned.

"That's one way of putting it. Amy divorced me after Paula called her and told her we were having an affair. We were married for five years. The first two were pretty good, the second two were awful and the last one…well, we'd given up by then. I haven't spoken to her in a long time. I just send her a check every month to pay off the property settlement. I'm almost done with that one, thank God."

CJ had her notebook out now and jotted down a few words. "And what about Missy?"

Clayton gave a big sigh. The waitress came to collect their plates and lifted an eyebrow at Clayton's half-finished meal. She glanced over at CJ as if to say "What did you do to get him off his feed?"

When she was gone, he answered, "I must have lost my mind with Missy, that's the only thing I can think of now. I was just so tired of the fighting with Paula, and then the iceberg treatment she gave me for months before she left that Missy was like, I dunno, fresh air. I fell hard for her and by the time I picked myself off the ground, we were married." He scrubbed his hand over his face again. "I'm sure payin' for it now. She's a bitch on wheels, I'm telling you."

CJ perked up. "Does she call you? Threaten you?"

He shrugged. "Kind of, I suppose. She's not any too happy with the money, but we weren't married very long and the increased value of the practice in that time didn't leave her much. Amy got a lot of it, and Paula got most of the leftovers. I work like a dog to pay off women I'm not even sleeping with anymore."

CJ fixed him with a steady look. "And support your daughter."

The coconut pie arrived, Clayton nodded his thanks and asked for a clean fork.

"Yeah. That's the only check I don't mind. She's a good kid, just moody like teenage girls can be." He took a bite of pie and some of the coconut flakes floated onto the tabletop like snowflakes. "You were moody at that age, if I remember right."

CJ put down her pen and grabbed her unused extra fork. She reached over and took a bite of pie.

"That's pretty good," she said.

"They get 'em from the bakery a couple a miles away."

She put her fork down again. One bite limit, that was the family rule. "I was a little moody, I guess," she acknowledged. "My hormones kicked in and dating boys wasn't getting it done. I didn't know what to do."

Clayton chewed thoughtfully. "Are we going to talk about it?" he asked.

"My hormones?"

He barked a laugh. "No. Why you left and haven't been back in all these years."

"I find it hard to believe you haven't discussed this at length with Mama."

"My discussion with Mama was limited to 'your sister's an evil homosexual and she's no longer welcome in our house.' But you didn't leave town for a year or two after that, right? So what happened?"

CJ sat back in the booth, studying him. He sounded curious rather than censorious.

"I told Mama and Father when I fell in love with another woman that I'd discovered I was a lesbian. That's when Mama threw me out. I went back to my girlfriend and we lived together until I found her cheating on me. So I packed up and left."

He nodded and again she had trouble reading his thoughts.

"You didn't even come back for Father's funeral."

She felt the sting of tears behind her eyes and blinked them back.

"Mama called Roger and told him to tell me I was not welcome. I considered it anyway, but Roger talked me out of it. He told me Mama was more than capable of making a major scene and Father deserved better than that. So I didn't come."

To her surprise, Clayton nodded again.

"He was right. She would've pitched a fit the town would still be talking about. I'm sorry that happened. Our father was a great man, and he should have had both his children there." Clayton shook his head. "Whatever else happened, he did love you, Belle. Even after you left, he'd talk about you to me when Mama wasn't around. He'd call Roger and get updates on you sometimes. That's how we found out you got married."

The conversation was taking a turn CJ couldn't have begun to anticipate. Was this her surly brother, the teenager who had made her life miserable for years? She didn't know what else to say, so she acknowledged, "Yes, I found the right woman."

He said dryly, "Congratulations. It's harder than it looks."

"Well, I didn't get it right the first time. Or the second, for that matter. But I got there."

"Are you happy?"

The tears threatened again. CJ said, "She's smart and serious and kind. And she really loves me. It hasn't always been easy, but yes, I'm very happy."

"I'm glad," he said and seemed to mean it. "I don't understand the whole gay thing at all, but I'm glad you're okay. I never wished you ill, I want you to know that."

She was going to cry if he kept this up. She said, "What about you, Clayton? You're with someone now, aren't you?"

"Yeah," he said. "Her name is Tayla. She's very nice."

"How did you meet?"

"Where else? At a bar downtown. She teaches third grade over at St. Joseph's. She was separated from her husband and starting to get back into the dating scene."

"Is this serious?"

He leaned across the tabletop at her.

"Look, stop poking around looking for suspects in my personal life, goddammit! I appreciate your help and all, but I'm not interested in being the subject of your investigation. And leave Amy out of this too. She's never done anything bad in her life."

She blinked at the sudden change in his mood. Could he really be a murderer after all? She responded mildly, "I'm not prying but there is only one really reliable way to get you out of this. I have to find at least one other more likely suspect, someone the jury, at least, will find more viable than you. And it wasn't some stranger off the street, Clayton. Whoever did this knows you. Or Amy. Period."

He slumped back, his sudden flare of anger spent.

"And you can't think of anyone who might have it in for you?" CJ persisted gently.

He shook his head. "I have to get back to work," he muttered.

"I'll call you later." CJ knew she wouldn't get anything more from him now. "And don't worry, I'll buy lunch."

Clayton nodded and slid out of the booth.

She watched him leave. She had thought she would know when she talked to him if he killed Amy or not.

She still had no idea.

The parking lot was almost empty at two thirty on a weekday afternoon. CJ rolled down the windows on her rental car, hoping to catch what breeze she could. She'd blissfully forgotten the humidity of her hometown in the years she'd lived in Colorado. It could get warm there but was never afflicted with the soul-sucking miasma of damp air that was surrounded Savannah. She could feel the hair on the back of her neck curling.

A white SUV swung into the parking lot. CJ took off her sunglasses. If she wanted to intimidate a witness, she often left them on. This was a witness she wanted to reassure, and nothing did that better than eye contact.

She got out of the car and waited patiently for the woman to approach her.

"Hello," the other woman said, her voice almost a whisper. Everything about her seemed small and faded, blond hair going gray, light cotton blouse, soft voice.

CJ extended her hand and gave her a business card.

"I'm CJ St. Clair. You're Miz Childs?"

She deliberately used the slurred pronunciation, covering all possibilities from Ms. to Miss to Mrs., an all-purpose Southern greeting for women above the age of twenty-one.

"Yes. I've got to pick up the kids in an hour, is that okay?"

"Of course. I appreciate y'all taking the time to meet me here. I know it must be hard on you."

Linn Childs looked at her in surprise. "Well, yes. Yes, it is."

"May we walk?"

CJ led the way out of the parking lot toward St. Paul's, a traditional white clapboard building with a slim, tall spire. At the top against the blue sky was a simple white cross. Even though it had been almost dark that night, perhaps Amy's eyes had been able to find the cross above her in that second before death. CJ hoped that it had given her a last moment of peace.

"So what do you want me to do?" Linn Childs asked nervously.

CJ said, "If you're willing, I want you to walk through what happened to you that night. I may ask questions, but I'll try not to interrupt too much."

Linn looked at her. "What happened to me? You mean what happened to Amy, right?"

CJ gently touched her arm. "It happened to you too. It was an awful thing to see and you have to remember that you were an innocent person caught up in this through no fault of yours. And I'm so, so sorry it happened."

To her dismay, Linn Childs burst into tears.

CJ managed to lead her to a bench in the grass. She put an arm around her shoulders and let her cry for a few minutes. After a while, Linn dug into her purse to find a tissue.

"I'm so sorry! I have no idea what made me fall apart like that."

"You don't need to apologize," CJ answered.

"It's just…no one ever said they were sorry for…me, you know?"

"I understand." CJ gave a mental demerit to the Savannah Chatham Metro Police Department. This was no way to treat a citizen who'd been through a traumatic event. Besides, treating your witnesses with compassion often got you the most information.

Assuming the witness wasn't involved, of course. CJ had no reason to think Linn Childs was anything but an innocent witness, but you never could be sure.

"Are you feeling up to this?" CJ asked.

"Yes. Yes, I think so."

"Sometimes it helps if you don't try to actually put yourself there again. Watch it happening as if you were watching a movie. It helps you detach a little bit."

"Okay." She dabbed at her eyes a final time and put the tissue away. "I'll try."

"Take me to the door you left from that night. How was the meeting?"

They talked through the evening. The meeting was as usual, perhaps running a bit later.

"Liz was there and she'd had a bad time of it lately, so we spent a lot of time helping her deal with the symptoms, you know, emotionally. Anyway, it was dusk when we finally broke up and we decided to walk out to the parking lot together."

"You and Amy were friends?"

Linn considered the question. "Yes and no. We met in the group, what, maybe eight months ago? We kind of hit it off. I have a girl about her daughter's age, you know how that is."

CJ nodded to keep the flow going.

"Anyway, we met for lunch a couple of times. We weren't like best friends or anything, but I liked her. She was nice."

"Yes," CJ agreed softly. "She was."

"So...we left about, I don't know, eight fifteen, I think. We walked out together down this way. No one was in front of us that I could see. There were still some women cleaning up inside from the meeting, putting the chairs back, that kind of thing."

They arrived at the curb and Linn took a deep breath.

"Amy's car was here," she pointed, "and mine was a couple of slots over. I don't know where he came from."

"Did he seem to appear in front of you? Behind you? Did he come from one side or the other?" CJ asked.

Linn stopped to consider. "Not behind us," she answered slowly. "He came from...you know, he could have been hiding behind my car. It's taller, see? He could have been crouching down, then come around the end. I think that's what happened. He came around and then he was there."

Lying in wait, whoever you were. Bastard.

"You're doing great," CJ reassured her. "Remember now, you're watching it. Just tell me what happened next."

She drew in and released a deep breath. "I was startled. I probably gasped or stepped back, probably both. Amy said something, I don't remember what exactly. Maybe only, 'What do you want?' Then I saw the gun and that's all I could look at."

"That's normal," CJ said. "It's logical to focus on whatever presents the most danger to you. Try to see more. Was he wearing gloves?"

Her eyes widened as CJ watched her fight for the memory.

"Uh…yes! Dark leather, black or dark brown. And one of those hooded sweatshirt things. I looked up at his face, but it was in shadow. The hood was pulled all the way forward."

"Compare his size to someone. How tall was he, would you say?"

"My husband is about six feet," Linn said. "He wasn't quite that tall. Maybe…" She eyed CJ. "Maybe your height, an inch or so taller. Not skinny, not fat, though it was hard to tell with that sweatshirt. It was a little big on him."

Well, it would have helped Clayton if the guy had been five foot six or six foot four. She hated average-sized suspects.

"Anything else? Pants, shoes? Any jewelry you could see?"

"Nothing shiny. Dark pants, I don't remember the shoes, although…" She paused.

"What?"

"Well, after…he ran away. There was something weird about the way he ran."

"Weird. Slowly? With a limp? Really fast? Zig zag?"

She shook her head. "None of those. Just…odd."

CJ left it for a moment. "All right. So he shows up in front of you and you see the gun. Where is it pointing?"

Linn suppressed a shudder and leaned against her vehicle. "Right at Amy. I don't think he ever even looked at me. He just pointed it at her."

"And what did he say?"

She stared off into the muggy afternoon for a moment. "One word: 'Purse.' He didn't even say 'Give me your purse.' Only the one word."

As if he didn't want you—or Amy—to hear his voice. "And what did you do?"

"I was just…frozen. I couldn't move, I couldn't speak. Amy took her purse off her shoulder and held it out to him. She said, 'Take it!', I think."

"Okay. Deep breath. What did he do?"

Now Linn shut her eyes. "He reached out with the hand not holding the gun—his left hand, so I guess the gun was in his right hand—and put it over his shoulder. Then he raised the gun a little bit. I thought he was going to tell us to run away, but he just aimed it at Amy and pulled the trigger. I've never heard anything so loud. Amy never made a sound. She fell backward. I thought…I thought he was going to shoot me too, but all he did was look at her a second, then ran away. I started screaming, I remember that."

"And you said he ran oddly."

She opened her eyes again. "Yes, I wish I could describe it better. Anyway, the women still inside the building came running out. They went to Amy, but we could tell right away she was gone. It was horrible. One minute we're chatting about our kids, and the next minute, the very next minute, Amy is dead. How can that be? What sense does that make?"

"You know what? It doesn't make any sense at all, Miz Childs. So thank you for your time and for going over this with me again. I don't think I'll need to bother you again, but I'll call you if I have another question. Meantime, may I make a suggestion?"

"Okay." She sounded hesitant.

CJ smiled at her. "Go pick up your kids and hug them. And kiss your husband when he gets home. Life can be very random, but the people we love make it worthwhile."

CHAPTER SIX

As Alex crossed the detective squad room, Lt. Frank Morelli called out to her.

"Hey, Captain, nice photo in the paper this morning."

Alex turned to see the laugh lines around his brown eyes deepening as he grinned at her. Across his desk, his partner Detective Chris Anderson's expression was better described as a smirk.

Alex stopped and crossed her arms. "What photograph would that be?"

Chris tossed her a folded paper, not the *Denver Post* but the Colfax weekly that concentrated on local news.

"Front page of the *Courier*. Pretty good article too, about the new memorial," she said.

Alex picked up the paper but didn't look at it. Instead she fixed both of them with her best boss glare.

"If I have somehow distributed the investigations workload in a way that permits you two to lounge around at this hour of the morning reading the paper, I'm sure I can find something else for you to do."

Frank laughed. Behind him, Detective Kelly called out, "I got a nice buncha second-degree burglaries for you if you need them, guys."

Chris made a face at him.

"That won't help our clearance rate any," she said. "No thanks."

Kelly laughed and returned to the report displayed on his computer screen. Alex said dryly, "Glad to see so much intrasquad cooperation. Now, how about we all get back to work?"

"Yes, Cap," Frank replied, still smiling. "But it really is a good article."

Alex retreated to her office and unfolded the paper. The photo was her official photograph in uniform, captain's bars shining against the navy-blue jacket. Her smile in the picture was restrained. The most usual uses for the official photo were when the officer in question was promoted, retired—or killed in the line of duty. In any event, she hadn't wanted to look too cheery.

She read the article while drinking her second cup of coffee. She remembered the interviewer, a young woman who seemed inordinately interested in the fact that Alex was a lesbian rather than concentrating on the theme of the piece. Fortunately, either the reporter or her editor had managed to get the article properly focused on the new memorial being dedicated in a couple of weeks.

Despite the fact that she was the chair of the memorial committee, Alex had assumed either the police chief or her immediate boss, Deputy Chief Paul Duncan, would be the speaker at the dedication. But Paul had made it clear that he had no interest in public speaking and he hadn't really given her much choice.

"It's for Charlie," he told her. "He'd want you to do it."

"Oh, that's not fair," Alex remembered telling him. "Dad's been dead for more than twenty-five years. You really think he'd care whether I pull the sheet off the granite?"

Paul was adamant. "It's for our fallen officers, and your father's name is on it, so write the speech."

And so she had, with CJ helping her refine it and cut it severely. Alex was determined to speak no longer than three minutes and she planned to rehearse the speech until she accomplished that goal. No one really wanted to sit in the park behind the police station on hard folding chairs and hear her talk. What she wanted was for people to acknowledge the cost of public service, the willingness of her colleagues to risk their lives every day they went to work.

She didn't think about her father often, but as she read she wondered if he'd be truly proud of her. She'd far exceeded his career achievements, but he'd never wanted to get out of the traffic division. He'd always said being a sergeant was the highest rank he ever cared to have. He liked being on the streets, driving and talking to people and being the first on the scene.

The reporter had included the story of her father's death, of course, the personal angle to her motivation to make the memorial a reality. It wasn't the best article she'd ever read, but it got the point across. She gave one last glance at the picture and decided to ask if she could keep the paper. CJ might want to see it, she supposed.

It was hunger that finally caused her to look up from an arrest report to see that the sky was beginning to darken. Lunch had been a long time ago. Alex packed up her desk, putting pending work into tidy piles, and took her jacket off the hanger on the back of her office door.

She got into her car, thinking about the days before she'd met CJ. Working until seven or eight o'clock every night had been her habit because there had been no reason to go home. Now CJ often called or came upstairs close to five every evening, talking about what to have for dinner or what movie to see. CJ's tastes were eclectic—she was equally happy at a jazz concert or munching popcorn at the latest Hollywood blockbuster. To Alex it seemed that she had been living in black-and-white before, and now with CJ her life was technicolor. Like Dorothy coming out of her house in *The Wizard of Oz*.

She stopped at the gate to exit the employee parking lot to wait for the automatic arm to lift. A glance in her rearview mirror told her Chris Anderson had been working late too. She and Frank had probably been out on an interview and he'd dropped her off to get her car. Alex lifted a hand in greeting and then pulled out to the street.

A screech of brakes alerted her a moment later. Someone in a Toyota sedan had cut Chris off by pulling away from the curb just behind Alex as Chris was trying to exit. Chris had managed to stop short of hitting the other car, although to Alex's eye another dent couldn't possibly be noticed. The sedan was still mostly blue with rust accents.

She could see Chris's aggrieved expression, but her detective waved her on. Alex drove off, the Toyota behind her and Chris turning for home the other direction.

At five minutes after nine that evening, Alex's phone rang. She set her book aside happily.

"Hi, sweetheart," Alex said. "How was your day?"

"Long," CJ admitted. "Everything all right there? What did you eat?"

Alex laughed a little. "You left enough for a month. Tonight I had my favorite."

"Ah. Clara Washington's famous meatloaf."

"Are you going to see her while you're there?" Alex asked. "Because if you do, you should tell her that her meatloaf sealed the marriage deal for you."

CJ's laughter made Alex feel warm down to her toes.

"Oh, darlin', I miss you already."

"I miss you, too, Red. Tell me how it went today. Did you see your brother?"

"I did. In some ways it went better than I could have hoped. In others…"

"Tell me," Alex urged her.

"He wasn't going off on me, that's the good part. I believe his words were that he 'didn't get the whole gay thing,' but he seemed more baffled by it than disturbed for some religious reason."

Alex wasn't sure how to react, so she settled for, "Okay, I guess. I mean, he's hardly on the moral high ground."

She could hear the amusement in CJ's voice. "Really? Why would you say that? Just because he's cheated on all three of his wives?"

"What are you sensing from him?"

"I wish I could figure it out. On the one hand, his claim that he's innocent seems genuine. On the other, he doesn't really want to consider who else it might have been. When I told him it was probably someone who knew him or Amy, he pretty much came unglued."

"You think he suspects someone?"

"I have no idea."

CJ recapped her other conversations. Summarizing the interviews aloud helped organize her thoughts, but some things remained elusive.

"I have a lot left to do," CJ concluded. "Tomorrow is ex-wife day, so we'll see how it goes. I'm also seeing his current girlfriend tomorrow afternoon. I'm hoping she can give me another point of view on Clayton. God knows I can use all the help I can get."

"I wish I could help you more," Alex said. "You said you think Clayton is hiding something?"

"I don't know. I have no idea if it's that, or if he's just so uncomfortable around me he seems off. It could be partly shock. I'm so frustrated that I can't read him better."

"Be patient. It's been a long time and you weren't close even when you were there. Have you talked to your mother?"

"Oh, yes. Mama would like to have hourly updates, so I'm answering about every third phone call. If I can't get her to back off a little, there will be a second murder in the family."

Alex said, "I'll get the bail money ready. Are you carrying?"

"No, there doesn't seem to be much point. It's in my hotel room, just in case."

Alex hesitated a moment.

"What?" CJ asked.

"I'd feel better if you'd take your gun," Alex admitted. "You don't know most of these people. And the chances are pretty good that you're going to talk to someone who was involved or knows who was. Do me a favor and think about it, okay?"

"All right, darlin'. I still have a lot of questions and not too many answers yet."

"It's always that way early. We have to figure out what the right questions are."

CJ sighed. "That's always the hard part. So much information and most of it's irrelevant."

"It'll get better soon, I hope. You've barely started."

"Talking to you always makes me feel better. Think you'll be able to sleep?"

"If I can't, I'll phone you and you can sing me a lullaby."

"That sounds kind of like fun. I'll call you tomorrow, same time, okay?"

"You can call me anytime. Sleep well."

"I love you, Irish."

"Me too."

"You ready for me, Paul?" Alex asked from the doorway of Deputy Chief Duncan's office.

He gestured her inside wordlessly and returned to his two-fingered typing, pecking at the keyboard like an old rooster plucking up corn from the dirt. Alex took her seat and waited for him to finish.

She'd known him her whole life. He'd been her father's closest friend while she was growing up and was her godfather. He and his wife had spent a lot of time with Alex and her sister when their mother died so young, and he'd helped Alex get a job with the department when Charlie had been killed on duty. Some of her success as a police officer—and as an adult, she supposed—was due to him.

He was fixed in her mind as he had looked when she was in her teens, the years she and Nicole spent three or four nights a week at the Duncan house having dinner. Every time she saw him lately she could see him aging before her eyes: his fingers gnarled and thick with arthritis, his waistline steadily expanding despite Betty's best efforts at changing his diet. His gleaming ebony head was smoothly shaved, but a few grizzled hairs had escaped his razor that morning.

Paul saved whatever document he had been working on with a sigh and turned to her. Lately his eyes seemed to be aging as well, the lids drooping lower than she remembered.

"How are you?" Alex asked.

He waved a hand. "Same old, same old. I don't suppose you'd like to take some carrots, celery and some kinda brown dip off my hands?"

Alex smiled at him. "Carrots, celery and brown stuff. Betty packing your lunches for you?"

He grunted. "That is not lunch. That is an afterschool snack for grade-schoolers. Lunch has meat and cheese and preferably something fried."

"Did you invite me up here to get me to buy you lunch? Because I'm not crossing your wife. I've seen her pissed off and I am not going there."

"Coward. No, that's not why I asked you to come in. Close the door, will you?"

Alex got up, trying to suppress her worry. Closed-door conferences were invariably bad news of some kind.

She returned to her seat and leaned onto his desk. "What's up?"

Paul leaned back and his chair moaned an objection to the weight shift.

"Nathan's taking a job out of state. Some kind of fancy consulting thing, probably pays a boatload of money."

"The chief is leaving? I hadn't heard anything. When?"

"End of next month. Official announcement is next Monday at the City Council meeting. He told me this morning."

Alex smoothed her fingers over the worn leather and bumpy stiches of the old baseball Paul kept on his desk, thinking fast.

"Are you thinking of applying?" she asked him. "Because you know you have my one hundred percent support."

He shifted again and the chair made another groan.

"I called Betty a while ago and she agreed. I was already thinking of putting in my papers next year."

"You're retiring?" Alex exclaimed.

"You don't have to sound so surprised. You thought I was gonna die in the harness? Betty wants to travel a little more and I think I'm ready. With Nathan leaving, it makes sense for me to get to break in the new chief and then ride off into the sunset."

"Paul, I don't know what to say. You deserve it, but yes, I am a little shocked."

"We were gonna invite you and Nicole and your nephew to dinner and talk about it, but I have a reason for talking to you now."

"Why?"

Paul reached over and took the baseball from Alex's fingers. His hands looked like big dark mitts. He looped his index finger and thumb on the ball like a pitcher testing his grip on a circle changeup.

"Because I want you to think about applying," he answered.

Alex sat back, the hard slats of the visitor's chair biting into her shoulder blades.

"You think I should apply for your job?"

"No. I think you should apply to be the new chief of police."

She had gone from surprise to shock to astonishment in a single conversation.

"You're not serious," she managed to say at last.

"Look. The city council is happy with us right now. Our numbers look good, the budget's under good control, your guys have solved a few high-profile cases in the last couple of years. They're willing to look internally, at least that's what Nathan tells me. You're the best candidate by a mile."

"You're not exactly objective, Paul."

"I am about this. Look, you don't need to decide anything right this minute, but you need to think about this long and hard. It's a great opportunity for you. Yeah, I know you're young, but it's time for you to make the jump if you want to. And I know you do want to."

Alex stared out of the window for a minute. Paul had a nice view of the park. Alex could see the base for the installation of the memorial she would soon be dedicating. The aspen leaves were on the cusp of changing color, barely beginning to fade from bright green to the characteristic gold.

Did she want to be the chief? The honest answer was yes. The thought of running the department was enticing to her beyond her ability to articulate. She had fallen into police work, but it suited her, the blend of structure and method and creativity. She could make Colfax PD into the premier department in the region.

But even assuming she could get the job, which was far from certain, there was an unavoidable consequence that barred her immediate acceptance.

"I know," Paul said, intercepting her thoughts. "But it's not like CJ couldn't find another job. She's a good cop, Alex. Roosevelt Sheriff's Office would take her back in three seconds, and if she doesn't want to go back there, I'll make some calls. Anybody would be happy to have her."

"You're kidding yourself, Paul. CJ is a great police officer, but you know a woman—a gay woman—in command levels in most cop shops is far from a done deal."

He met her eyes. "Yeah. Black cops, female cops, gay cops, I get it. But any department who didn't want her isn't a department you want her to work for. Anybody good will give her a job."

Alex hoped that was true, but that wasn't the point at this moment.

"I have to talk to her, Paul. You know she's out of town, and I'm not sure I want to discuss this with her over the telephone."

"How's that thing going? Family problem, right?"

They'd kept the real reason for CJ's trip home deliberately vague. CJ didn't want department gossip to feature her brother's murder charge.

"So far so good, I think," Alex answered. "I'm not sure how long she'll be gone yet, but we'll talk about it."

"I'll keep an eye on the council's application process and the time frames for you," Paul promised.

Alex stood. "Paul, I want you to know how much I appreciate everything you've done for me. My career is due in part to you being my mentor and I want you to know how much that meant to me. I..."

Paul hoisted himself out of the chair, which sighed in relief. He lumbered around the desk and embraced her in a rare show of emotion at work.

"I'm proud of you, Captain Ryan. And I'll tell you, your dad would have been bursting his buttons with you. He would."

"Thanks, Paul," Alex murmured into his uniform shirt. "I'm going to miss you."

"No, you're not. Sunday dinners will be mandatory from retirement onward, so plan on it. If you two don't show up, Betty will issue a subpoena or send a squad car over for you."

"I told you I wasn't going to risk Betty's temper. It's a deal. Oh, and Paul? That brown stuff in your lunch?"

"Yeah?"

"It's ground up chickpeas. They call it hummus. Try it, it's pretty good stuff."

He gave her a skeptical look. "Uh-huh. I bet it's especially good spread on the bun of my cheeseburger."

CHAPTER SEVEN

The fitness center at her hotel held no appeal for CJ in the morning. After rejecting her mother's repeated demands that she stay at her family home during the trip, she'd booked herself into the Bay Inn on the bluffs above the Savannah River. Her morning's exercise was a brisk not-quite-a-jog down Factor's Walk, the riverside street that ran along the old brick buildings near the Cotton Exchange. For years the Savannah Cotton Exchange had set the prices for the world's supply of cotton, negotiated by the cotton brokers, the factors who represented the buyers and sellers of the bales that lined the wharves on the river.

Now the cotton offices were shops and restaurants, pulling in tourists to walk on cobblestone streets and gaze at pieces of the history of the South. CJ was proud of her city and its history, but she never forgot that much of it was built on the back of slavery.

The water was gray today. Downriver, CJ could see the ferry crossing from the convention center across the river on

Hutchinson Island. She'd gotten a window table at Conroy's Pub because her meeting was before the lunch rush. The pub was in a former cotton warehouse and the house bar drink was actually called the Cotton Gin. CJ settled for iced tea and was happy that she remembered to order unsweet tea.

CJ watched the hostess point toward her table for the benefit of a woman who was dressed in a nice cream-colored suit. CJ stood as she approached.

The woman offered her hand. "I'm Paula Prendergast."

"CJ St. Clair. Thanks for meeting me before the place fills up."

Paula slid into the booth. "Yes, you have to show up before eleven forty-five or after one thirty to get a table." She gazed for a moment out the window and added, "Especially one with a view."

CJ studied her as Paula glanced at the menu. She was remarkably well-assembled, perfect French manicure and what looked to be an expensive haircut that had her hair feathered around her narrow face. She looked nothing like Amy, and CJ wondered a moment whether Clayton had chosen her because she was different.

They gave their orders and CJ asked, "What do you do, if you don't mind my asking?"

"Real estate agent with Antebellum Properties. It's been going well." CJ imagined so, given that the woman was wearing a five-hundred-dollar linen suit and shoes that cost at least that much.

"I'm glad," CJ said. "I know some women don't manage coming out of a divorce successfully."

She waited to see what reaction this generalization would produce.

Paula looked wryly amused.

"I'm sure that's true," she remarked. "I was certainly struggling for a couple of years, but that was during the marriage. Once the divorce was in the works, everything got better. Your brother is a mess. No offense."

CJ was hardly going to argue with her. "You sound remarkably calm about it."

Paula shrugged. "It was a long time ago, or it seems like it now. If I'd been a little smarter, I'd have settled for having an affair with him. That part was fun. The rest of it…"

CJ drank more tea and waited.

Paula rapped a bright white nail edge on the tabletop. "Look, what do you want to know? I know Clay is in a boatload of trouble right now, but I have no idea what you're looking for from me. I don't know anything about it."

CJ leaned back and opened her arms to look as nonthreatening as possible.

"I'm trying to find out what happened to Amy," CJ said. "I haven't seen my brother for years and I don't know him well. It's sad to admit that but it's true. Anything you can tell me about him—his relationships, his money issues, anything that might help me understand him would help me. And him."

Paula unfolded her napkin and arranged her knife, fork and spoon carefully.

"Why would you think I'd be interested in helping him?"

"If you're not," CJ said mildly, "then why did you come?"

Paula smiled, revealing the first flaw in her perfect presentation: a slightly askew canine tooth.

"Maybe I was just curious to see what the queer sister looked like."

CJ kept her face expressionless.

"Well?" she said after a moment. "What's the verdict?"

Paula chuckled a little. "Well, aren't you bold as brass? Ever think of selling real estate? Bet I could make you into a best-seller."

"Not my area of interest, but thanks. You didn't answer the question."

It was Paula's turn to ease back against the booth cushions. She actually looked CJ up and down again. CJ felt her eyes narrow despite her best efforts.

"You're wearing a wedding ring," Paula said.

"I'm married," CJ answered neutrally, still wondering where Paula was headed in the conversation.

"To another woman?"

"Yes, that's the way lesbians do things."

Paula laughed aloud. CJ waited for the next remark.

"She look like you?" Paula asked.

If she had been on the job, this line of questioning would never have begun. But now CJ was curious. Was this headed toward an anti-gay diatribe? Because it didn't feel that way.

"Not particularly. She's shorter than I am, very dark hair, pale skin with blue eyes. Black Irish, they call it. But that's not what you mean, is it?"

"No. You like butch girls?"

Well, that was unexpected. "We seem to have wandered from our original topic quite a way. Any particular reason we're talking about this?"

Paula shrugged. "Just curious. I don't suppose you're like Clayton."

"In what way?"

"You know. The wandering type."

The waitress reappeared and refilled CJ's glass of tea. Paula ordered a second drink, and CJ wondered if she always drank in the middle of a workday or only when she was propositioning women who were strangers to her.

It had been a while since a woman had actually made a pass at her. She'd seen a few glance her way, but she felt very married and thought perhaps she was projecting an "I'm taken" air. If she did, Paula Prendergast seemed comfortable ignoring it.

"I'm not, actually," she said. "The wandering type. And if I were, I can assure you I would avoid any woman who had previously slept with my brother."

Paula seemed unconcerned by her reaction.

"Just checking," she said. "I like a little change of pace every so often. And whatever Clay fouled up in his life, which was plenty, he was really good in bed. Thought you might have the family trait."

Mercifully lunch arrived at that moment. CJ had promised herself a few local treats on this trip and today's meal was a crispy scored flounder with an apricot shallot sauce over creamy grits and collard greens. The first forkful fulfilled her happy anticipation: the fried fish was succulent, the sauce both sweet and a little spicy. It would be a bowl of soup for dinner, she figured, but this meal was worth it.

CJ said, "Now that we've got that out of the way, are you willing to talk with me about Clayton?"

"Why not? The thing is, Clay is always looking for the next thing. He likes gadgets, new cars or the latest laptop, whatever. And I didn't know it at the time, but he's like that with women. He likes the romance, the pursuit, the sneaking around. Once the ring is on your finger, he starts to lose interest. If Clay were in charge of the world, wives would be like cell phones: you could go to the store and get a new model every year or two."

"I'm guessing you didn't figure that out until later."

"Of course not. Let me tell you something I'm sure you don't know, seeing as how you don't sleep with men. Every woman who has an affair with a married man thinks he'll never cheat on her the way he's cheating on his wife. Because you think, 'I'm different. I'm special. He'll never want someone else once he has me.'" She sighed. "What a crock. Cheaters cheat. Sounds like a bad country song, doesn't it?"

"A little," CJ said. "And that's what happened between you and Clayton?"

"Yes, I was stupid enough to play both parts. Mistress who broke up his marriage and then the lousy wife who made him cheat on me with someone else. I thought it was love, so I called Amy and told her Clayton was in love with me but was afraid to leave her."

"How did she take that?"

"How do you think? She didn't believe me, she was hurt, she was furious. She'd been having some kind of physical problem, which turned out to be multiple sclerosis. I didn't care, I just wanted Clay. So I got him and he ended up paying through the nose: support for his kid, alimony or whatever they call it now for Amy and of course she got a lot of money in the property settlement because the practice was doing so well."

"I've heard he's having money problems now."

Paula wiped her mouth with her napkin. "I wouldn't know. He's paying me, but I didn't get much compared to Amy. By then I didn't really care. I only wanted out."

"Were you upset that you didn't get more?"

She put down her fork a moment. "Look, the money helped me get my real estate license and I'm doing great. I'm probably making as much as Clay is now but either way, I just don't care. In fact, that pretty much summarizes my feelings about Clay: I just don't care about him one way or the other. We had a good fling, a bad marriage and it was a long time ago now. He's in my rearview mirror."

CJ finished her meal and crossed her knife and fork neatly across the plate.

"Where were you the night Amy was killed?"

"The cops asked me that. I was with a client until about seven forty. I could have gotten across town, I guess, but they seemed satisfied that it would have taken a jet plane to get me there. I was on Tybee Island."

CJ digested this information. Her alibi witness might have mistaken the time, but Paula would have had a difficult drive to the church by a little after eight o'clock.

"Do you own a gun?" CJ asked.

"The cops asked me that too. Yes, I drive around by myself to meet strangers, sometimes at night. I have a thirty-two caliber semiautomatic in my glove compartment. I showed it to the cops." She pushed her own plate away.

"Look," she said, "I never hated Amy. She was in my way, that was all. I wouldn't have killed her years ago, so I had no reason to do it now. And I don't hate Clay enough to try to implicate him after all this time. I told you. When it comes to Clay, I don't give a damn anymore."

St. Joseph's Catholic School had a classic antebellum look: white columns framing the two-story neo-Greek building. The parking lot was tucked behind the building so as not to ruin the park-like effect of the front grass. It was a lawn worthy of watching Scarlett O'Hara run down in her ball gown to meet Ashley Wilkes. All CJ could think about was the herd of lawnmowers it would take to keep it neat.

She found Tayla Newman outside as they'd arranged on the phone. It saved CJ from having to run the gauntlet of security that surrounded the school campus.

Tayla was sitting on a bench that overlooked the playground, which was crowded with children running, playing and generally making noise. Tayla rose to meet her, and CJ found herself looking directly into her face. It was the rare woman who was as tall as she, but Tayla was easily her height. She was casually dressed in cotton pants and a colorful print shirt. Her dark hair was pulled back from an attractive face. Younger than Clayton, CJ guessed, maybe mid-thirties. She regarded CJ with big, dark eyes.

They exchanged introductions and Tayla said, "Sit down, will you? I've only got a few minutes and if I don't eat something I'm out of energy in an hour."

"I imagine they keep you running. Third grade, right?"

"Yes. Jesus, eight-year-olds, they're like those fish you read about. They're always nibbling at you all the time."

That was an interesting way of thinking about it, CJ thought.

"Thanks for taking the time."

Tayla scooped yogurt into her mouth. "Clayton asked me to. He said you're trying to find out who killed his ex."

"Well, I'm at least trying to help his defense case."

Tayla threw her a sharp sideways look. "How're you going to do that? It looks bad to me."

"Did Clayton say that?"

"No, he's acting like it's a traffic ticket or something. Frankly I think he's being stupid about it."

"I tend to agree. You don't sound like you're from Georgia."

"Oh, no. Pennsylvania originally. Met my husband at college, and we moved down here."

"The weather's quite a bit different, I imagine."

"The summers are miserable, but there's no snow to shovel. And being by the water's nice. Anyway, what can I tell you? I wish I'd stayed over that night, but I had a curriculum meeting the next day, and I had a lot of prep to do." She ate more yogurt.

"How long have you known Clayton?"

"We met, um, eight or nine months ago? Yes, right after New Year's. That's about right. I kicked my soon-to-be-ex-husband to the curb as a Christmas present to myself and was starting to go out with some friends. I saw Clayton at Wet Willie's and we just clicked. You know how it is."

The first time CJ had seen Alex was at a crime scene. A suspect had taken a couple of shots at her detectives trying to serve a warrant and Alex had taken charge of the search for the fleeing man. Everything about Alex drew her in: her looks, her serious demeanor, her calm presence. CJ had known in the first minute that Alex was someone she wanted to know better.

"He was still with Missy," Tayla continued. "But you can't stop love. They split up a couple of months later. We'll be getting married as soon as our divorces are finalized."

That was interesting news. Clayton hadn't mentioned it to her.

"Any ideas who might have a grudge against Clayton?" CJ asked.

Tayla finished the cup of yogurt and put it back into a paper bag next to her on the bench.

"That's an easy question. Missy hates him with every bone in her cosmetically enhanced little body. She can't stand that I took him away from her. This is totally up her alley."

"You think she would still have access to his car?"

"Oh, please. He rarely bothers to lock it, even at work. Anybody who knows what he drives could plant the gun there. Even Missy could scrape together enough brain cells to arrange this."

"Why would she kill Amy?" CJ asked.

Tayla shrugged. "Amy is the target where Clayton had the motive, that's all. It could have been his partner just as easily. Amy was probably easier to get to, that's all."

"You've given this some thought," CJ observed.

"I told you, Clayton isn't taking this seriously enough. I'm glad you're here now; maybe he'll listen to you. He certainly hasn't been listening to me." Tayla stood up. "I've got to get back to the little monsters. Let me know how it's going, will you?"

"I will. By the way, do you own a gun?"

"No, my ex was the gun nut. He kept them all when we split. Why are you asking? Do you think I killed Amy?"

"I don't know. Did you?"

Tayla shrugged. "If I wanted to kill somebody, it would have been Missy. She is a twenty-four seven, three sixty-five bitch. I've got to get back to the monsters. I'll see you later."

CJ watched her go back toward the building and wondered why a woman who clearly didn't care much for children was teaching them.

As CJ pulled out of the school parking lot, her cell phone rang. She'd taken the time to sync it to the Bluetooth in her rental car, so she punched the hands-free button on the steering wheel and said, "CJ St. Clair."

"Hi. This is Melissa. You left me a message, about a meeting today?"

It took CJ a moment to remember that Melissa was Missy's proper name. Maybe she'd gone back to it after she and Clayton split up.

"Yes, thanks for calling me back. I'd like to talk to you about Clayton."

"And why the fuck would I want to do that? Especially with his sister?"

The venom from her voice filled the car and made CJ want to open the windows to let it out.

"I'd appreciate an hour of your time anyway," CJ said. "I'm happy to meet you whenever and wherever you'd like. I'll buy lunch if you want. I'm trying to get some information about what happened to Amy."

"Same question. Why the fuck would I care about the first wife? Ancient history."

CJ was getting a little weary of everyone telling her how the past was no longer relevant.

"Melissa, I know you and Clayton are getting a divorce. I'm guessing he treated you not very well, and I'd like to hear about that and anything else you want to tell me about him."

CJ could hear her weighing the advantages of an audience for her grievances against having to meet with her. Finally she could hear a sigh.

"Oh, all right. There's a bar on West Bay, the River Tavern. I can meet you tomorrow at four if you can find it."

It was only a few blocks from her hotel. CJ said, "Great. Thanks for doing this, Melissa. I'll see you then."

It looked as if the rest of her afternoon was free, and CJ knew immediately where she wanted to go. She turned the car around to go back through downtown and pick up the Harry S Truman Parkway. On the way there she made a phone call. She knew she'd be welcome, but no properly brought up lady dropped in unannounced.

The Avondale neighborhood was far from the sweeping lawn and white pillars of St. Joseph's Catholic School. The houses here could best be described as bungalows, many of them with classic Craftsman details: wood trim and small front porches featuring the ubiquitous rockers for sitting out in the evenings. Most of the shrubs and gardens were neatly tended and there were trees everywhere.

CJ turned the wheel a few times to avoid the worst of the potholes. Mixed in with the tidy homes were some derelicts, front yards given up to weeds and plants choked off with the deadly kudzu vines, the "vine that ate the South." She spotted a few gang tags here and there on the clapboard sidings.

She found the house after double-checking the address. It was painted bright white, its porch invitingly shady. A hanging porch swing beckoned her from across the flawless grass that looked as if every blade had been trimmed by hand.

Actually, knowing Mason, perhaps it had.

Before CJ could actually set foot on the grass, the front door swung open and a small, round African-American woman came out onto the steps. She was wearing a plain blue cotton apron over a light print dress and on her feet were blindingly white Keds.

In a world where everything had changed about home, it filled CJ with joy to see her there. Apron, Keds, the smell of delicious cooking wafting from the door and the same welcoming smile was all she needed.

"Get in this house, child!" Clara Washington said.

If Roger Thornton had connected her to her family's past, Clara connected CJ to herself. Her mother had been alternatively demanding and indifferent to her as a child, but Clara always seemed to see her as she was. Clara had shared her love of cooking and reading with a little girl, and CJ knew how much Clara's love and acceptance had shaped her into the woman she had become.

CJ wrapped her arms around Clara. She could smell the scent of rosemary clinging to her. It smelled of roast chicken for Sunday dinner, potatoes mashed by hand with red-eye gravy and collard greens.

"Now you stand there and let me fill up on looking at you. You are looking fit and fine, I must say."

CJ laughed. "Not too fit, my doctor says."

Clara shook an admonishing finger at her. "None of that talk in this house, you know better. What I see is that you are settled in to yourself in a happy life. Isn't that so?"

CJ linked arms with her to walk them back into the air-conditioned house. "Yes, ma'am. You are right as always."

Clara laughed and CJ realized that Clara had taught her how to do that too. Or maybe she'd already known how and Clara had been the one to give her permission.

The small living room was spotlessly clean. A soft upholstered sofa looked worn at the arms, but there was no speck of dust on the old coffee table, which was anchored by twin piles of reading material: books on one end, magazines on the other. On each end of the couch was a newish-looking brass floor lamp.

Clara said, "We like to sit here of an evening and do our catching up. Mason is always reading those silly sports things about football and baseball and such. He's in some kind of deal where they pick out players and bet on them or some foolish thing."

CJ grinned. "It's called a fantasy league. Individuals draft specific players or teams and compete against each other to see how well their selections performed."

Snorting, Clara said, "Fantasy! Bunch of old men trying to waste time. Been married almost a half a century to that man and he's still as lazy as the day I met him."

CJ was well-versed in this bit of marital byplay. Mason, who had held two or three jobs most of his life and manicured the lawn and gardens meticulously, was lazy. Clara, who could assemble a dinner for eight from a sack of cornmeal and a hambone, was a terrible cook.

"Well, sit down, child. Lemonade on the way."

CJ settled herself into the embrace of the sofa. She picked up the top book in the stack on Clara's end of the couch. *Rebecca*, by Daphne du Maurier. Clara loved rereading her favorite classics.

Clara returned with a tray bearing tall glasses filled with ice and the lemonade pitcher. To her delight CJ spotted a plate of cookies.

"Tell me those are your shortbreads," CJ said, hope brightening her voice.

"Of course they're my shortbreads," Clara replied. "You were sneaking into the kitchen to steal them from the cooling rack as soon as you were tall enough to reach the counter."

CJ shook her head. "No, it was as soon as I could figure out how to pull over that footstool you used to keep in the kitchen to reach the upper shelves."

"Lord have mercy, you were always into something, from the time you could walk."

The lemonade was the perfect sweet-tart blend. "Is there anything more refreshing than lemonade on a hot day?" CJ asked.

"I suppose not. Now you're going to sit right there and tell me every little thing I want to know. It's been dog's years since I've seen you face-to-face."

"In that case, I need a cookie first."

The cookie tasted of creamy butter and sweetness and crumbled onto her tongue. CJ made a blissful sound.

"Mine never turn out to be this good," she complained. "And I'm using your recipe."

Clara shook her head sorrowfully. "You just didn't get that cookie blessing, poor child."

"Maybe not," CJ conceded. "But luckily, I did get the meatloaf right."

"Well, that's good."

"Alex said to tell you it was the reason she married me. Well, I think she was pretty serious anyway, but the meatloaf was the pièce de résistance."

Clara chortled and munched on her own cookie.

"My, these did turn out well. Well, honey, I'm always glad to help in the romance department, as you know. Giving Ella my special fried chicken recipe did the trick on that slow-moving man of hers. They're getting married next June."

"That's great! And how's Matt doing?"

Clara grabbed her phone to show her a couple of pictures. "He's up to Petty Officer Second Class. Won't be long before he's running that boat. Meantime he's seeing places I could only dream about."

CJ said gently, "You can go, you know that. Anywhere you want to, I'll send you and Mason."

She shook her head. "Belle, you've been more generous than you needed to be with us. You'll have to come in and see the stove you bought. Six burners, all the bells and whistles."

CJ sat still, thinking. She'd offered to get them out of the neighborhood many times, but Clara was clear that Avondale was home and she was staying put until they carried her out. CJ had been forced to settle for the new stove and the air-conditioning unit that was humming away, keeping the living room nice and cool.

"Where's Mason? In the back?"

Another snort from Clara.

"He's doing what that man does best, wasting time. He's taken to going down to the fire department, of all things. I bake and he takes them cupcakes or banana bread or cookies and then he sits around and chews on the newest center fielder or watching some episode of football or some such. He'll be home directly. The man never misses dinner, I promise you that."

"Despite the fact you're a terrible cook," CJ teased her.

"Yes, he eats like a field hand after he's been sitting around on his backside all day and then complains about the food. Enough about him. Tell me how you are."

CJ summarized her life in a few sentences, answering every question Clara had. When Clara seemed satisfied, she took another cookie and said, "Tell me about Clayton. I've been worried sick about that boy since I read about him in the papers. I called your mama, of course. She was her usual self."

"Sorry to hear that. She came to see me in Colorado and asked for my help."

"Lord have mercy. And how are you doing?"

CJ leaned forward. "If I ask you something, will you tell me the truth?"

"I am offended that you think I wouldn't."

"But you're a kind person and I want to know what you really think."

Clara finished her lemonade.

"You ask me, child. You want to know if I think Clayton did this terrible thing."

"Yes."

She refilled her glass slowly and jostled the ice cubes around so they clinked against the sides of the glass. Somewhere outside CJ heard someone starting up a lawnmower.

"When you were growing up, Clayton wasn't really mean. But he was selfish always. He wanted what he wanted and no one else mattered much. I thought his daddy might have been able to help him but you know the doctor was always busy saving other people instead of paying attention to his own family." She gave CJ a compassionate smile. "I'm sorry to say that, but it's true."

Yes, CJ did know. She adored her father, but he was like a visitor in their lives, a kindly man who dropped in occasionally for a birthday party or dinner.

"So what are you saying, Clara?"

"The Clayton I knew, if someone got between him and what he wanted, he didn't care. Remember the time he pushed you off the swing?"

"I still have the scar on my knee."

"You were wailing like a baby at feeding time. As I recollect, I had to bring you inside and feed you cookies 'til you stopped howling."

CJ smiled. "Chocolate chips."

Clara patted her hand with her own work-worn one.

"Food just about always worked on you, child."

CJ said, "It still does. Though actually it wasn't the food so much. It was that you made it for me. You know when I left and moved to Colorado, you were what I really missed the most. You were always home to me, Clara."

To her surprise she saw Clara's eyes misting over. Clara was kind, but she was also a practical and hardheaded woman. CJ couldn't remember the last time she'd seen her cry.

Clara blinked the tears away before they could spill. She cleared her throat and said, "You know James Baldwin? I believe he once said that home might not be a place but an 'irrevocable position.'"

"My favorite quote about home is from Robert Frost. Home is where 'when you have to go there, they have to take you in.'"

"'Take you in.' I like that."

"Me too."

Alex glanced at the display on her office phone when it rang and saw Paul Duncan's name.

"Hello, Chief," she answered.

"Go close your door, Alex," he instructed her.

She did so, thinking that now they had graduated from closed-door meetings to closed-door telephone conversations. A couple of her detectives glanced up curiously but returned to their work.

"What's going on?" she asked.

"I got some information for you. About the, ah, opening."

"Yes?" He was being so circumspect Alex wanted to laugh. Did he think the department's phones were bugged?

"Looks like they're going to start taking applications first of the month. The council says they're going to do a 'nationwide search,' but they always say that. You know Councilman Ruiz always wants to hire in-state people. And Councilwoman Snodgrass is lobbying for a woman or person of color, so there's that. You still thinking about this?"

"I'm thinking, Paul. But it's a lot about CJ at this point, and I really don't want to get too heavily invested until we've had a chance to talk."

"Yeah, I get it. But maybe you could at least start the conversation with her while she's gone? I mean, she's gonna need time to think about it too and you said yourself you don't know how long she's gonna be away."

Alex leaned back in her chair. "What's really going on, Paul? What's the rush?"

She listened to his heavy breathing for a few seconds.

"Look," he said at last. "Here's the thing. I have to have some surgery."

"Paul! What's going on?"

"It's nothing. Hernia. But the thing is, they're telling me I could be out for six weeks. I can put it off for a little while, but I'd really like to get the new chief in here before I'm out for so long. You can hit the ground running, you know? If I knew they were gonna make the right decision…"

Alex interrupted him. "Paul, this is silly. Your health is the most important thing. Get the surgery scheduled. We'll survive. Don't make me call Betty."

"I've already talked to her about this. She's not real thrilled waiting on the surgery, but she's okay. It can wait for a while. But it would really make me feel better if you could decide what you wanted to do."

"You're not giving me a lot of room here to say no."

"That's not true. I just want to know one way or another. If I have to call a couple of people, I have some backup plans. But you're my first choice by a mile."

"You sound like you're going to be making the decision."

"No, of course not. But Nathan did let me know I'm writing the qualifications and I know I'll be on the initial interview committee. I'm gonna make sure that there is someone we want as a finalist for the council."

"Okay," Alex said. "I'll talk to CJ. But I'm not going to rush her or rush myself."

"I understand. But let me know, will you? Soon as you decide, let me know."

CHAPTER EIGHT

Saturday morning errand day didn't seem as much fun for Alex without CJ waiting at home. She decided to give herself a treat and went to her favorite independent bookstore, browsing the shelves with coffee in hand. She found a new Marcia Muller mystery and decided to try a new author in paperback. With the relaxed air of someone who had no appointments to keep, she even looked in newly released nonfiction to see if there was anything CJ would like. Deciding to take a chance she picked up a biography of Daphne du Maurier, the author stuck in her head after CJ told her about the visit to Clara Washington.

CJ had stayed for dinner at the Washington house, and she told Alex later they spent the evening reliving every childhood memory she could dig up. Alex's favorite story was the pony, rented for Clayton's birthday party, who ate the birthday cake while he was opening his presents.

"What did you think of the ex-wives?" Alex asked her.

"I haven't met Missy yet. She's not too thrilled about meeting me, but I promised to listen to all the bad things she had to say about Clayton so I'm meeting her at a bar tonight. The other two interviews were…interesting."

"Tell me more," Alex said.

"The current girlfriend is a third-grade schoolteacher at the local Catholic school. She's pretty but not what I'd call a shy and retiring type. Of course, she's a Yankee, so that would explain it," CJ said.

"Hey, wait a minute."

"You're not a Yankee, darlin'," CJ explained soothingly. "You're a Westerner. Totally different thing."

"Oh. Okay," Alex said, mollified. "So what was your impression?"

"She told me she thinks Clayton is taking this whole thing too lightly, so we agreed on that. We didn't have a lot of time, but she clearly wanted to know what was going on. She couldn't really help me much. On our next conversation, I need to ask her about her husband."

"Come on, CJ, she's married? What the hell?"

"I know. She says she kicked her husband out before she met Clayton, but I wonder. I also wonder if that doesn't give him a big ole fat motive."

"Could be. How about the other ex?"

"Paula. That was interesting, too, in a different way."

"How so?"

"Among other reasons because she made a pass at me."

"She…did what?"

"Yep. I believe she said something like she enjoyed a change of pace from time to time."

"Tempted?" Alex said it lightly but noticed her grip on the telephone had tightened. CJ was the best-looking woman she'd ever personally met, and everything about her seemed to attract women and men both.

CJ responded immediately.

"Oh, hell no. Totally putting aside the major ick factor of the fact that she slept with Clayton, I am a happily married woman, thank you very much. I understand that it can take more than one try to find the right relationship, but Clayton seems to leave a trail of marital destruction behind him like Sherman marching through Georgia. By my conservative count, between his marriages and other people's marriages, he's responsible for at least five divorces."

Alex said mildly, "He had help."

"Of course. I'm not letting the women off the hook, but here's the point. Someone hated him enough to do this and I don't have a couple of suspects, I've got a riverboat full of them."

"Maybe we're attacking from the wrong angle here," Alex suggested. "Maybe this really was about Amy and Clayton was merely a convenient patsy."

"I know that's a real possibility. It just doesn't feel that way. Anyway, I've got a couple of more people to see Monday, but on Sunday I'm going to see Laura."

"Are you worried?"

"Worried. Eager. Hopeful and terrified. That about sums it up. We're having brunch at Clayton's house."

"Could be worse. Could be at your mother's house."

Alex could almost hear the shudder over the phone line.

"No, that's later on Sunday afternoon. We're having a nice mother-daughter tea for the updates. It was the only way I could get her to stop calling me every seven minutes."

"I believe the term 'glutton for punishment' was invented for this very situation. CJ, are you going to be all right? I could fly out, you know."

CJ laughed. "For tea with Mother? Oh, no darlin'. It's proof of my undying love for you that I wouldn't let you do it even if you could. Don't worry. When I get back to the hotel Sunday evening, I will have a nice bottle of chardonnay on ice waiting for me."

"Try not to drink it all in one sitting."

"It won't be easy. What's up with you?"

As the bookstore clerk bagged her purchases, Alex still felt guilty about hiding the news about the chief of police opening from her partner, but CJ sounded tired and discouraged and Alex decided not to bring it up. Now knowing that CJ was facing her family on Sunday, she wondered if she could bring it up at all. Surely next week would be soon enough.

When she neared her SUV in the parking lot, Alex hit the remote open and put the bag of books in the back. As she backed out of the spot, she silently cursed the city planners that let developers build tiny parking spaces for giant vehicles. The next moment she laughed at herself. All she had to do was drive something normal, but CJ had firm ideas about the heft of a vehicle suitable to protect her. Alex could hardly argue; her prior car had probably saved her life in a rollover accident.

She edged carefully out into the aisle, trying not to tap the bumper of the car parked across the lane behind her. Another glance in her rearview mirror caused her to brake.

It was a beat-up blue Toyota with rust accents. Alex remembered seeing it before, just outside the police parking lot a few days ago.

An odd coincidence. Or was it? Denver was a big city and this had to be the same car. What were the chances Alex would see it twice in that period of time?

It was probably nothing, but Alex didn't like coincidences. She scrambled for a pen and jotted down the license plate number on a napkin. Someone behind her honked and she cleared the aisle.

Was someone following her? And if so, who was it?

At four o'clock on a Saturday, the River Tavern was full of people watching college football on the dozen or so big screens scattered around. CJ loved football but didn't care for beer or noise. Her idea of a great football-watching experience was hosting friends in her home, having homemade snacks where people could cheer as loudly as they wanted without worrying about disturbing others.

She sighed. She would attribute her lack of interest in sports bars generally to encroaching middle age, but in truth she'd never liked loud, boozy parties. For one thing she was always much too interested in what was actually going on in the game.

A large group clattered out, high-fiving each other as they went. One of the games must have ended. Most of the Southeastern Conference games would be over by now, but fans of the Mountain and Pacific time zone teams were just getting warmed up.

This time her interviewee had beaten her there. Melissa was sitting at a table with a man, leaning against him. There was a mostly empty pitcher of beer in front of them.

CJ said, "Hi. I'm CJ. Thanks for meeting me." Melissa already knew who she was, and she decided not to remind her by using her last name.

Melissa looked up and said, "Oh, you're here. Well, siddown. I'm Missy."

CJ wondered if she used both names interchangeably or if Missy was her name when she was a little drunk. The man next to her gave CJ the eye up and down, so CJ returned the favor, which seemed to give him a second of discomfort. Whoever he was he was wearing the Southern good ole boy uniform of jeans, graphic T-shirt featuring the country band Florida Georgia Line and a beat-up red baseball cap featuring the logo of Harvester International, a manufacturer of tractors and other farming equipment. She figured his feet, out of sight under the tabletop, were clad in cowboy boots. From a glance at his hands, she doubted he'd ever stepped in cow shit or climbed on a tractor in his life.

Missy was in her own outfit suitable for the bar, tight T-shirt with a scoop neck to show off what were her considerable assets. CJ remembered Tayla's cutting reference to Missy's surgically enhanced body. These breasts certainly were not original equipment for her otherwise petite frame. CJ tried not to stare, but they were an impressive set and they were generously featured.

"This is Donny." Missy waved a hand in introduction. "Donny, this is the prick's sister. You know, the queer."

"Well, hell, honey, you don't look like no queer." Donny smirked.

CJ had heard this one before and she ran through her responses in her mind.

And you would know this because you hang out with lesbians yourself? I'm not surprised.

What do queers look like exactly, since you're an expert on the subject?

Well, since I am a queer, you obviously have no idea what you're talking about, do you?

None of these responses would probably help the interview go smoothly, so CJ settled for, "Looks like you could use another pitcher, Donny. Here, it's on me."

He opened his mouth, then shut it again, revealing a need for some serious dental work on a couple of those incisors in the process. He took the twenty CJ offered. She figured that was probably at least twice the price of the pitcher and that she would not be receiving change.

He stuffed the bill into his pocket, scooped up the pitcher and said, "Be right back, babe."

Missy said, "Bring us some popcorn too."

"Yeah, okay." He didn't sound enthusiastic.

CJ preferred her interview subjects to be sober and alone when she questioned them. She couldn't get Missy to undrink whatever beer she'd had, but at least she had a couple of minutes alone with her.

"Thanks for meeting me," she began.

"You said you wanted to hear all about the prick, right? Thas what I call him, the prick. 'Cause he is one."

"Tell me what he did," CJ said.

"What'd he do? Ev'rything." She twirled a strand of hair, predictably bleached blond, around her finger. "He seduced me, thas what he did. He made me break up with my boyfriend and then after we got married he just dumped me flat. No money, no nothing. He's a prick."

Yes, a prick. Got it, she thought. "How long were you together?"

"How long?" This question seemed to strain her thinking and she twirled another strand. She was going to ruin the effect of the teasing and hair products.

A memory of a remark Clara had once made about a friend of her mother's hit her. 'Big hair, closer to God.' CJ struggled to keep her face still.

"We were married 'bout a year, I guess. I was seein' him before that."

"When he was still married to Paula."

That remark earned her a glare. "They was *separated*," she explained indignantly.

"Yes, right. So what happened?"

"He was so good lookin' and he knew how to treat me, y'know? I mean, most guys, it's just a quick suck off in the back of the car, but he took me to a real nice motel and ev'rything."

CJ was glad she hadn't been drinking anything at that moment. Well, it would take a while to get that picture out of her head.

"So he divorced Paula and you two got married. Did he ever talk about his ex-wives?"

"Never 'bout Paula. He always said she was a cold-hearted bitch. Amy, he was okay with her. They had a kid, y'know. I was kinda jazzed 'bout being a stepmommy, but she didn't seem to like me much. I bet she thought I was taking her daddy away from her."

CJ could think of a few other reasons why Laura might not be fond of Missy. "They got along all right?"

"Yeah. Seemed to. We'd go over and pick up—what was her name?"

"Laura."

"That's it, Laura." Missy seemed to be ever-so-slightly sobering up. "And Amy always seemed kinda nice. She was never mean to me anyway. Not like my folks, they used to fight like cats and dogs."

"So what went wrong between you and Clayton?" She took a quick glance toward the bar. Donny was busy talking to another guy while the popcorn popper behind the bar rattled merrily away.

Missy dropped her hand from her head and shrugged.

"I'll be damned if I know. One minute we were fucking and the next he was telling me to pack up."

I really needed to stop hearing about Clayton's sex life, CJ thought. "Do you remember when that was?"

Donny was on his way back to the table, hands full of pitcher and a basket of popcorn. "Um, lemme think. Oh, yeah, it was right around my birthday, the bastard. March 26."

As Donny made his way through the football fans, CJ did some mental math. Clayton had met Tayla right after the first of the year. He hadn't broken up with Missy until almost three months later. That was interesting.

She wondered how long it would be before he started cheating on Tayla, assuming he wasn't in prison.

Donny announced, "Didn't have another hand to get you a glass."

CJ gave him her best fake smile. "That's all right. I don't need a beer. So how long have you two known each other?"

"Fourth of July party," Missy answered quickly. "Remember, honey?"

Donny poured beer. "Oh yeah, I remember. We had some fireworks that night, didn't we?"

She giggled and rewarded him with a lean toward him that gave him a good look down her cleavage. He acknowledged the effort with a suitable leer.

CJ managed not to roll her eyes. CJ had a couple of close male friends, but there were days when all she could do was wonder why anyone could feel an attraction to men. So many of them were, well, clueless about women. Not for the first time in her life, she sent a little prayer of thanks heavenward that God had seen fit to bless her with loving women.

"USC is kicking some serious ass," he remarked. "Dykes like football and stuff, don't they?"

She wanted to slap him. "Here's a couple of tips for you, Donny. Many lesbians find the word 'dyke' offensive, particularly when used by a guy, so I'd drop it if I were you. If you're not careful you might just run into one who will do to you what the Trojans are doing to their opponent today."

While he was still processing that comment, she continued. "And you might stop making generalizations about gay people generally, since you apparently have no idea what you're talking about."

She rose. Donny lifted his beer and spat the word, "Bitch!"

"Wow, snappy comeback, Donny. You really need to do some vocabulary work there."

CJ picked up her purse, but Donny had a last parting shot.

"I hope they fry your brother for killing that girl!"

She turned back to them. "Why do you care? Or did you kill her yourself to get some revenge on Clayton for Missy? Did she put you up to it?"

CJ got another view of his dental deficiencies. *He really should learn to keep his mouth shut*, she thought, *in more ways than one*.

Missy jumped in. "You're an awful person! I would never, ever do anything like that!"

"Where were you the night Amy was killed?"

"We were together, all night!" Missy exclaimed. "Right, Donny?"

He drank more beer. "Don't tell this bitch anything else."

"That's not much of an alibi," CJ pointed out. "I imagine we'll be having another conversation, Missy. Good talk."

CHAPTER NINE

Clayton lived on Skidaway Island, one of the most exclusive communities in the state of Georgia. It was cut off from the mainland by rivers, the Wilmington on one side and the Skidaway River on the other. CJ drove south on the Harry S Truman, then made her way over the Diamond Causeway. Once on the island, the houses were a scattered variety of ranchers, traditional antebellum and contemporary. As always, the yards were filled with trees and shrubs, many sporting autumnal flower displays of yellow and orange chrysanthemums.

The sultry weather had broken overnight, and CJ stepped out onto the driveway into a pleasantly warm morning. She'd never been here before. When she left Georgia, Clayton and Amy were living in midtown, not too far from Clayton's practice.

He must have bought this when the dental practice took off, she thought. If this wasn't a million-dollar house, she'd be quite surprised. It was a big mid-century modern, all glass and flat planes on the roofline. The landscaping had been professionally done, the greenery integrated nicely with the shape of the house.

She rang the doorbell and a moment later Clayton appeared. He seemed more relaxed than at their lunch at the diner. He was wearing shorts originally colored brick red which had faded to nearly pink. He had on deck shoes without socks and a light-yellow piqué polo shirt left untucked.

"Come on in," he greeted her. "Laura's still in her bedroom, talking on the phone. I gave her five minutes to finish up."

Just a casual little family brunch, she thought, eating with people she'd never met or hadn't seen in years.

The living space was as large as she'd guessed it might be. The floors were Savannah gray brick, with a complementary light gray slab of granite surrounding a modern-looking gas fireplace. The furniture was mid-century too. A square, low-profile sofa stood on thin metal legs, flanked by two chairs in the same style but a different shade of gray fabric. There were touches of color in merlot pillows. The look was so cohesive that CJ assumed he must have had an interior designer put it together.

But a second glance told her that there were things missing from the setting. On two spots CJ could see where art had been removed. In one instance it had been replaced by a print that didn't match the design scheme, an ordinary seascape with blues and greens. On the other wall, the painting or art piece hadn't been replaced at all, leaving a hole like a gap in a picket fence.

Had he sold some things when the money got tight? CJ wondered what the mortgage on the house looked like.

"It was nice this morning, so I thought we'd eat outside. Will you get the tray from the kitchen island? It's that way. I've got to turn the chicken on the grill."

"Of course."

The kitchen carried out the living room scheme, with white cabinets and a subtle gray herringbone backsplash. CJ took the tray with a large salad already assembled in a bowl out to the patio.

"The chicken smells great," CJ said.

"Yeah, I like to grill. I like it when my clothes get all smoky. It gets old, all that antiseptic stuff I do at work. I wash my hands twenty times a day. I think it's my way of rebelling."

"Well, I get that. I like cooking myself."

"I'm not surprised. You were always hanging around Clara in the kitchen when we were growing up."

How much honesty could he take? "That's true. I liked it there."

He manipulated the tongs and turned over the chicken breasts.

"And I get that. It was away from Mama," he said.

She had no time to respond. A young woman stepped out onto the patio, punching off her cell phone as she walked.

CJ had wondered if Laura would look like Amy or the St. Clairs. The answer was neither and both. She was average height, with light brown hair and eyes the color of milk chocolate. She still carried a layer of what her mama used to call baby fat, but she had almost outgrown the awkward coltish stage of adolescence. She had on denim shorts and a T-shirt that proclaimed she'd gotten it at Abercrombie & Fitch. She was barefoot.

Clayton looked down and frowned. "I asked you to put on shoes."

"It's the patio, Dad. I don't need shoes for the patio."

She turned toward CJ and said, "You're here."

"I am," CJ said. "It's been a long time."

Laura frowned. "Like my whole life."

"Not quite," CJ replied, smiling. "I held you the day you were born. I was at your first birthday party."

Laura turned to her father.

"You didn't tell me that," she said, her voice accusing.

Clayton shrugged.

"The chicken is ready," he said. "Let's eat."

Laura sat down across from CJ, nursing an aggrieved air. *This is not going to be easy*, CJ thought.

She dished up salad onto the plates, and Clayton distributed the chicken breasts on top.

"Dressing, Dad?" Laura asked.

"Oh, sorry. I forgot." He got up and went into the house.

Laura gave CJ a direct look. "Are you really my Aunt Belle?"

What was this? "Yes. I go by CJ now. And I'm really your father's sister, cross my heart."

Laura gave a short nod. "Good," she said. "So you can get me the hell out of here."

Clayton stepped back out onto the patio, juggling three bottles of dressing.

"I wasn't sure which one we wanted," he said, apology in his voice. "So I brought them all. We've got ranch, Italian or French."

Laura gave a perfect sigh of appalled dismay.

"Italian dressing, Dad. Who puts ranch on chicken?"

Lots of people, CJ thought, *but we are all so very sure of everything at fifteen.*

He passed them the Italian dressing and sat down again.

"So who was that on the phone?" he asked as he cut up his chicken. "Was it Brian?"

"No, it wasn't Brian."

"Well, who was it then?"

Another sigh. "It was a girl from school, Dad. We're working on a project."

"For biology? Or chemistry?"

"Other classes have projects too, you know. Not only science."

"So what was it then?"

"World history."

"What's it about?"

"Dad, stop with the third degree already! You know, I've been managing to get through high school just fine up until now without you micromanaging everything I'm doing. Okay?"

Clayton threw a look, then lifted his hands.

"Sorry," he said to CJ, then turned back to Laura. "It's not very polite to be rude to me in front of your aunt, somebody you just met."

Laura threw down her napkin. "Don't apologize for me, Dad! I'm not being rude. You're being a pain."

CJ said calmly, "She's right, Clayton. You really shouldn't apologize for her. She's old enough to be responsible for her own behavior." She took a bite and after swallowing added to Laura, "And you were not exactly *not* being rude."

CJ expected her niece to storm off, but instead she folded her arms.

"What does that mean?" she asked.

"You made him cross-examine you instead of answering his question," CJ pointed out. "You can't manipulate him into asking you several times and then complain about it. Either tell him the first time or explain to him why you're not going to tell him. If you're tired of him asking you every little thing, volunteer the information you're going to give him and tell him how you feel. That would be the adult way of handling it."

CJ watched her think about that. Using the word "adult" struck at her self-esteem.

After a minute Laura picked up her fork again and resumed her lunch.

Score one for the good guys.

As she ate her meal, CJ wondered what was really going on in Laura's mind. She had to be still grieving for Amy. Losing her mother so young was always going to be more or less a lifelong sorrow. She'd seen it in Alex, where it manifested as a bone-deep yearning for connection with someone, the desire for another heart to make a home.

She smiled at the thought that she'd brought Alex a home at last.

"What are you thinking about?" Laura demanded.

"Laura!" Clayton exclaimed.

"It's all right," CJ said. "I forgot kids are either watching our every move or ignoring us completely. If you really want to know, I was thinking about my partner."

"Dad says you're a lesbian."

"I am."

"So are you, like, married?"

"I'm exactly married."

"What does she look like?"

CJ remembered the same question from Paula Prendergast a few days ago, but this time she got out her phone and pulled up some photos. She passed the phone across the table.

Laura stared at the picture of Alex for a minute, then swiped over to see a few others.

"Who's the little boy?" she asked. "Is he yours?"

"That's Charlie, our nephew. He's the son of Alex's sister. She's a widow, so we try to spend a lot of time with him."

"He's cute," Laura said, handing the phone back. "And your wife, she's…well, I wouldn't say cute, exactly. More like she looks really smart."

CJ smiled. "She is really smart. And nice."

Laura nodded. Her cell phone chirped the theme from *The Pink Panther*.

Clayton frowned. "Laura, you know the rule. No calls at the dinner table."

"This isn't the dinner table," she answered, pushing back her chair.

"Yo," she said into the phone as she went back inside the house. Clayton glared after her.

A bit at a loss, CJ said, "The *Pink Panther* music is pretty retro."

"What? Oh, yeah. I think I met the girl who's calling. She has very pink hair."

"Makes sense, then. Want me to help you clean up?"

"No," he answered, waving a hand in dismissal of the dirty dishes. "It's Laura's job. She'll have to come back out to do it."

They sat for a minute in the pleasant shade, the birds having a lively conversation of chirps and squawks.

"So how's it going?" Clayton asked her. "Have you found anything out?"

"It's little early for any conclusions. Have you thought of anything else?"

He sighed. "You took me by surprise at the diner that day. I hadn't really thought about how it looks. But somebody actually put the gun in my car and went to the trouble of wearing a jacket just like one I own. Who would do that? I've been thinking about it since we talked."

CJ said, "You know Missy hates you quite a bit."

He sighed. "Yeah. She was a mistake from the beginning."

"Did you know she has a new boyfriend?"

He sat up straighter. "I didn't know. Does he look like a possibility?"

"Not unless she helped him. I doubt he could mastermind anything more complicated than brushing his teeth. Which I suspect he does badly."

"It could be Missy, I guess. Though it's hard to believe."

"Let me ask you about someone else. Have you ever met Tayla's husband?"

"No. She said he was a lazy jerk, kept going from job to job. He was out of the picture before we met."

"I'm going to track him down anyway. He's the most recent person, other than Missy, who might feel injured by your activities."

He gave a bitter little laugh. "'Activities' is the nice way of putting it. You mean my screwing around. Did you see Paula too?"

CJ said, "I did. And if she has it in for you, she's doing a great job hiding it. She told me she doesn't feel anything about you one way or the other, and I think I believe her."

"That's probably true. That happened while we were still married. So what's next?"

"I'll keep at it. Was Amy working?"

"At home. She was doing some freelance technical writing. I think I've got her boss's contact information somewhere."

"Send me a text when you find it. I'd like to talk to him. If it was someone from Amy's life who killed her, he might have something that will help me. And if it's okay with you," she added as she stood, "I'd like to go say goodbye to Laura."

Laura was lying on her bed, her cell phone resting on her stomach. CJ said, "May I come in a minute?"

"Sure."

"I wanted to say goodbye. I'm due at your grandmother's house for tea in a while."

Laura made a face. "Oh, I bet that'll be fun. Is she as mean to you as she is to my dad?"

"Until a couple of weeks ago she refused to talk to me at all. How is she mean to your father?"

"Always runs him down. No matter what he does, it's never good enough. Dad told me she threw you out of the family for being gay."

"Pretty much."

"I think that's stupid. It's not like you can help it."

"You're right about that. So…I think you should tell me what you meant."

Laura's eyes shifted away to the comforter on her bed.

"What do you mean?"

"I'm not playing twenty questions with you like your father does," CJ said. "Tell me what you meant when you asked me to get you out of here or don't tell me. I'm not going to play games."

"Dad told me you're a cop. You talk like one."

"Have you talked to a lot of cops?"

"Nah. But I watch *Law and Order* sometimes."

"That's not necessarily the real deal. And you're changing the subject."

Laura still wouldn't look at her. She gazed around her room, which had the unlived-in look of a part-time residence. She hadn't lived here, CJ realized. She was only here on weekends before her mother was killed.

"I'm glad we met face-to-face," CJ said. "I'll call you if you give me your cell number and maybe I can see you again before I leave."

"Wait a minute."

CJ remained standing.

Every emotion was visible across Laura's face. In one moment she seemed to be a child again, fearful and uncertain. The next second she seemed resolute and very grown-up. CJ watched the silent war until Laura said, "I'm scared."

CJ sat down on the bed.

"You'd be pretty foolish not to be," she said.

Laura looked surprised. "Really?"

"Really. You lost your mom. Your father might be going to prison. You can't do anything about the whole situation and that's terrifying. I'm so sorry, Laura."

"I...I'm just..." She bit her lip. "What if they convict Dad? They'll really put him away somewhere, won't they?"

"Yes, very likely."

"Then...oh, my God, they'll send me to live with Grandmother. And I can't take that, I really can't."

CJ covered her hand with her own.

"Listen carefully to me. If you don't want that, then we won't let it happen. You're borrowing trouble before it gets here, okay? If things get really bad, I..." CJ took a deep breath. "We'll come back and get you."

"You'd do that? Let me live with you?"

"I'll have to talk to Alex, but yes. We'll figure it out. I promise."

Laura took a deep shuddering breath. CJ watched a little of the tension go out of her.

CJ took Laura's cell phone and punched in her own number.

"Call me anytime," she said. "If you need to talk, I'm here. And do me a favor. Try to be a little patient with your dad. He's under a lot of strain right now."

Laura fingered the cell phone for a minute. "Dad said you're trying to help him find out what happened."

"Yes, I am."

She took another deep breath. "I know something. It's not much, but I don't think anybody else knows."

CJ felt her pulse kick up a notch. "Okay."

"Mom was seeing someone, I think. Like dating somebody, I'm pretty sure. For a couple of months before..." Her voice trailed off.

"Why do you say that?"

"A couple of times I'd get home and she'd be late getting back. And she was sort of dressed up, you know? Like she'd been out. And once I caught her on the phone when I came into the room and she said, 'I have to go.' Like you do when you don't want the other person to know who you've been talking to."

"Did you ask her about it?"

"One time. She said it was too early to talk about, but that she'd tell me when the time was right. That's all I know about it."

"Think a minute. Did she give you any idea who it might be?"

Laura wrinkled her forehead in concentration.

"I think…I think he must have dropped her off one of those times. I heard the car engine. It sounded like one of those sports cars. But I didn't see it. I don't know who it was. Does that help at all?"

"It does help, Laura. Truly. If you think of anything else or if you just need to talk, please call me."

"Okay. Can I call you Aunt CJ?"

"I'd like that."

It was a long drive back across town to her mother's house in Ardsley Park. The Sunday traffic wasn't bad, which was partly to CJ's regret. A nice accident snarling up the freeways and making her an hour or two late for tea wouldn't have been a bad thing.

But she arrived at the neighborhood on time. She drove around Chatham Crescent next to Tiedeman Park, not far from the First Presbyterian Church she had attended growing up. The church looked pretty much the same, gray-beige brick surrounding narrow Gothic-style windows and doors. The white trim looked freshly painted.

Tiedeman Park was filled with dog walkers and people playing Frisbee in the mild afternoon. An old man and an ancient basset hound were on the grass and CJ couldn't decide which one was shuffling more slowly.

She drove down her street, seeing the changes in houses and yards. She waited to feel the tug of homesickness, the sense of nostalgia at being back home. Some things she did miss: everything was green, there were trees everywhere and the houses themselves had a settled look, as if they had belonged to the landscape for decades.

But the deep emotional chords she expected to play were silent. It was both home and not home, the place she was from but not the place she belonged. The sights, sounds, and smells of the city had pleased her. The familiarity of black and white faces, the tastes of the food, the rivers and parks soothed her memories of growing up without triggering a longing to return forever. She was surprised and relieved. Leaving again would not be hard. She had told Alex that Alex's home was her home and it was true. She missed the beautiful Rocky Mountains and the cool dry air. In just a few weeks the aspen would be at their shimmering golden peak.

CJ smiled to herself as she parked her car in her mother's driveway. She would be home in plenty of time for the two of them to take a drive into the mountains some weekend to enjoy the aspen forests at their height. They would hike and CJ would take pictures. Maybe they could take Charlie this time.

As she reached the front door, it was opened by a man she'd never seen before. He was dark-skinned and his curly hair was closely cropped. He was wearing a dress shirt and slacks with a crisp and spotless white apron.

"Miz St. Clair," he greeted her in a deep voice. "Welcome. Your mother is waiting for you."

CJ stepped into the foyer. "Thank you. I don't believe we've met."

"I'm Charles," he answered as if that were a sufficient explanation.

The foyer had been redecorated. The hall tree had been replaced with a gold foil mirror and Louis XIV table. The tile flooring had been removed and in its place was a pale marble. From her glance into the living room, CJ could see a similar transformation: the leather couches and wooden side tables were gone, the substitutes carrying out the style set in the foyer with brocaded fabric upholstery, carved and fluted wooden legs on the chairs and tables. The rug was different too. The only thing CJ recognized in the room was the last family portrait she remembered: her high school graduation, the four St. Clairs smiling stiffly for the photographer.

Had they ever been the happy family in that picture, really?

"Ma'am?" Charles interrupted her reverie.

"Sorry. Yes, I'm ready."

Charles ushered her into what her mother always called the breakfast room.

Her mother was already seated at the table. There was a white tablecloth laid over the glass top and if there were more than two chairs with the set, they had been removed. It looked to be quite the tête-à-tête.

"There you are," Lydia St. Clair announced. "Sit down."

Nice to see you too, Mother.

Come on now. Breathe. You can be civil to her for an hour.

CJ took the other chair and smoothed the napkin over her lap.

Lydia said, "We're ready, Charles."

Charles reappeared bearing a tea tray with an old-fashioned silver teapot, creamer, sugar and silver spoons neatly laid out on a fresh linen cloth. The silver bore no hint of tarnish. CJ wondered how many hours Charles had spent polishing it to its gleaming silver sheen.

"Pour out, Belle," Lydia said.

CJ put a thin slice of lemon on her mother's saucer and put two sugar cubes in her own cup with the delicate silver tongs provided.

"Well?" Lydia began. "Did you see Clayton today?"

"I had lunch with him and Laura."

"I told him Laura should stay here, what with all the turmoil going on at his house."

"There's no turmoil there, Mama. He's out on bond, it's not like there are police sitting in his living room."

Her mother shifted restlessly at the contradiction. "I'm sure he's very distraught."

"He's worried certainly. He should be. Mama, you need to prepare yourself for the possibility that he may be convicted."

"I refuse to consider it. That's why you're here, Belle. You have to resolve this."

CJ sipped at her tea, just barely cool enough not to burn her tongue. She mused on why she liked her hot tea sweet but her iced tea without sugar. Lydia eased the slice of lemon into her teacup and stirred the liquid to cool it, the spoon making tiny clinking sounds against the fine china.

Charles returned with a plate of petit fours in yellow, pink and green icing decorated with delicate miniature flowers.

"Thank you," CJ said to him. "Charles, have you worked for Mother a long time?"

She saw her mother's lips purse in disapproval at the question. You spoke to servants to give them direction and that was all.

"About four years," he answered. "Do you need anything else, Miz St. Clair?"

Lydia said, "That will be all, Charles."

He nodded and slipped silently away.

CJ selected a yellow petit four and bit into it. It was lemon, tart and sweet. The flavor reminded her of Clara's homemade lemonade.

"You hired him after Daddy died," she said conversationally.

"Charles is irrelevant to this conversation," she replied, her tone dismissive.

But CJ wasn't done yet.

"Is he your driver as well? Because I'm fairly certain he didn't make these delicious cakes. I can see the box from Le Petite Cakebox on the kitchen island. And you hired a limo in Denver."

"I'm perfectly fine, Belle, and you are prying into matters that don't concern you."

She reached for her teacup and knocked it askew, sloshing tea into her saucer.

CJ reached for a napkin to soak up the spilled liquid.

"Leave it," Lydia said. "Charles will clean it up later."

"How's your eyesight, Mama?" CJ asked quietly.

"What on earth are you…"

"Just tell me."

Lydia reached for her cup again, more carefully. She sipped at it and then managed to return it to her saucer.

"Cataracts. My ophthalmologist says surgery is simple, but I've been so busy. It's nothing."

CJ drank her own tea. Finally she said, "If you'd like, I'll fly back when you have it done. To make sure you're all right."

"Belle, I don't want to discuss this. I want to know about Clayton's case."

CJ summarized everything she'd been doing for the last few days. Lydia, surprisingly, listened without interruption until the end.

"So who did this?" Lydia demanded.

"I don't know, Mama. I have a lot of work left to do."

"Well, you'd better get to it. Clayton's reputation is at stake here. And I can't imagine what effect this will have on Laura's future if he's convicted. It's bad enough she will have the stigma of her mother being murdered, of all things. It's bad enough that her father has been divorced three times or that you…"

Lydia stopped abruptly and CJ finished the sentence for her.

"Or that her aunt is a lesbian?"

Lydia's mouth compressed until her lips were nearly invisible.

CJ folded her napkin and stood up.

"Yes, I'm sure all of that will have a terrible impact on Laura's debut into society and her shot at landing a suitable law student or future investment banker for her lovely wedding to some scion of a great Southern family," CJ said bitterly. "But at least you've still got a chance with her, since I'm a lost cause."

"Belle, sit down. We're not finished."

"Yes, Mama, we are. I have work to do. Thank you for the tea and cakes. They were lovely. And Mama? Don't call me anymore. If I find something out, I'll call you."

CJ sat in her car in the driveway, trying to calm down before driving back to the hotel. Why did she let her mother trigger her like that? Families knew all your soft spots, the places that would bleed when poked.

Lovers were like that too, CJ mused. But you chose your lovers at least. Your families were the burden you bore whether you wanted them or not.

Her phone buzzed with an incoming text. Seeing Alex's name made her smile.

How's your day going? If you need rescuing, I can be having an emergency.

CJ smiled. She typed a response.

Just escaped. Driving back to hotel now, will call you when I get there. Love you.

Love you too came the immediate response.

She turned the car on, but before she put it into reverse another text came through.

It was from Clayton with the information about Amy's employer. Now she'd have something else to put on tomorrow's schedule.

Surely things were going to start making sense soon.

CHAPTER TEN

As the Monday morning detective squad meeting broke up, Alex stopped Frank Morelli.

"I'm wondering if you'd do me a favor," Alex asked him.

"Of course, Cap," he answered promptly. "What's up?"

She handed him the napkin where she'd written down the number of the Toyota on Saturday and told him the story.

"Run the plate for me, will you? I've got a meeting that will probably run into lunch and I'd like to find out who owns the car."

"Sure thing. You want me to check on the owner too?"

"Whatever you find out. I'd love to know if the guy has a sheet."

"You got it. Happy meeting."

Alex groaned. "It's the first budget planning meeting. It will last for hours and it won't be the last. Just shoot me now."

Frank grinned. "Nope. If I shoot you, then I'll be the boss and I'll have to go to the budget meeting. Forget it."

On the way upstairs, it occurred to Alex that Frank might be closer to being the boss than he thought. She'd been grooming him for a while, urging him to get promoted, trying to plan for her successor. He was methodical and mature and he got his paperwork done, all good signs for a head of detectives. Was he enough of a leader? It wasn't easy to tell. Sometimes he seemed a bit too easygoing for the job. But he'd done well helping tame his partner. Chris Anderson had been an undisciplined if talented officer, and now she and Frank were Alex's most solid team. In a way, she hated to break them up. But maybe Chris was ready to mentor someone else now. She'd certainly settled down, found a good woman to live with and had proven to be an inspired investigator.

Budget meeting. Alex sighed and went into the conference room armed with next year's projections.

They broke the meeting a little after one o'clock, and Alex was starving. She went downstairs into her office to dump her file folder and grab her jacket.

Frank appeared in her doorway. "Good meeting, Cap?"

"They're never good. The best ones are tedious, the worst ones are agonizing. Unless you have a ham and cheese sandwich in your hand, you should get out of my way."

"Whoa! I know better than to get between a woman and her lunch. I just wanted to let you know what I found on that plate."

Alex sat back down. Her curiosity trumped her hunger.

"You have my full attention, Lieutenant."

He sat down and began to read from the printouts in his hands.

"Car is a 1999 Toyota Corolla, registered to a Shaylynn Goetz, current address 321 Webster in Denver."

"Not Colfax. Interesting. What else do you know?"

"She's got a few things on her sheet. A drunk and disorderly when she was a kid, a DUI arrest almost twenty years ago that was knocked down to DWAI and another DUI that got her some jail time a few years after that. She's been clean for the last dozen years or so, looks like. Might have been one of those people who spend their twenties getting wasted and then grow up, maybe."

"How old is she?"

"Um, looks like forty-two."

Alex swiveled her chair around and stared out her window.

"I'm guessing you don't know her," Frank said. "And I did check, all the arrests but one were in Denver and you weren't the arresting officer on the one Colfax charge."

"You're right, I've never heard of her. Do you have her driver's license photo?"

He handed it over and she looked at it. It showed an ordinary-looking white woman with lank brown hair and dull eyes. Alex had never seen her before.

"This is weird. Maybe she's got a relative or boyfriend who's the link. Damned if I can figure it out," Alex said.

Frank heaved himself out of his chair. "Now I'm curious too. In my spare time, I'd like to dig around a little more."

Alex said, "Okay, thanks. Maybe it was just a coincidence after all."

He grinned at her again. "Oh, come on now, Cap. Good detectives don't believe in coincidences."

"But they still happen."

"Yeah, but if they do, it's just a coincidence."

Alex snorted at him. "Get out of my office, Morelli. I'm going to lunch."

The office building CJ located was tucked into a suburban area behind a strip mall that featured a sandwich shop, beauty parlor and a couple of franchises that served fast food. The building itself looked well-kept if plain. She supposed the rent was quite reasonable.

She found Educational Toys Inc. on the second floor. There was a small outer office, but no one was in it.

"Hello?" she called out.

A black man emerged from the inner office. "Oh, sorry, she's out. Can I help you?"

"I'm looking for Brady."

"That's me. You Miz St. Clair?"

They sat together in his office. It was barely big enough for his fake wood desk, a metal filing cabinet and his desk chair. It wasn't quite big enough for the chair he pulled over from the small waiting area for CJ to sit in. She was really sitting in his doorway.

"Sorry. We hardly ever get any visitors. Just a manufacturer's rep sometimes, like that. You said on the phone you wanted to talk about Amy? You're not a cop?"

"I am, but not in Georgia," CJ explained. "I'm working privately on Amy's murder, trying to develop information the police might have missed."

He regarded her thoughtfully.

"Private," he repeated. "Wait, you're working for the guy who was accused, aren't you? You can get out of here right now."

CJ stayed put.

"I am working for him," she admitted. "But before you throw me out I'd like to tell you two things."

"Yeah?" His tone was not receptive.

"The man who was accused of the murder is my brother."

He chewed on this a moment, then shook his head.

"Then I'm sorry for you. I understand family and all, but I'm not interested in seeing whoever killed Amy get off."

"The second thing I want to tell you is that I knew Amy. She was married to my brother and she was the mother of my niece. I liked her very much and I want to see whoever did this to her pay for it."

He stared at her. "Even if it's your own brother?"

"I'll tell you candidly I don't think he did it. But if he did, yes, I hope he pays the price for it. Amy was a good person and no one deserves to die like that."

He continued to look at her. Finally he picked up his pencil and said, "Are you just shining me on with this so I'll talk to you?"

"I'm hoping you'll talk to me, but I'm telling you the truth."

He pushed the pencil around the desk a moment.

"You're right," he said at length. "She was a very nice person. Ask your questions."

"How long did Amy work for you?"

"I pulled out her file after you called. I hired her first time two years ago for a specific project. I liked her work so we sent her more things over time. She was freelancing, you understand, but once I saw what she could do I sent her plenty of work. I don't think she had any other clients for the last year or so."

"What did she do for you, exactly?"

Brady spread his hands.

"Everything, really. If it required writing I sent it to her. She did our letters, our instruction manuals, even helped write our employee manual."

Did he need an employee manual for two people? Brady read her face and said, "This is just the office. We've got a manufacturing plant with forty-two employees in Pooler. We make and sell toys and ship them all over the region. Amy was part of our team and I'm real sad that she's passed away."

"Did she come in for meetings, to the office or the plant?"

Shaking his head, Brady answered, "No, ma'am. I gave her a tour of the factory once, but we did everything by email or phone, pretty much. I probably didn't see her more than three times in all the time I knew her. But we talked on the phone about once a week. She was always real nice."

"How did you find her?"

"An online posting."

"I don't suppose you know who she might have been seeing?"

He frowned. "You mean, like dating? No idea. I knew she sometimes had some physical problems, but she always got her work in on time. Although…now as I think about it…"

"Yes?" CJ said encouragingly.

"The last couple of months, when I talked to her, she seemed…I'd say happier. More upbeat, kind of more cheerful. Like something good was going on in her life."

Something good, CJ thought. What was it? A new man? And was he the reason she was killed?

CJ stopped at the sandwich shop near Brady's office and picked up sandwiches and chips before she drove to Clayton's professional building. His practice was south of Ardsley Park in one of the nicer suburban areas. She supposed he needed to be near a good supply of people with money who wanted straight, white teeth.

The waiting room was spectacularly nice for a dentist's office. Dark hardwood floors set off a bright salmon color on the walls. The receptionist's desk was a brushed aluminum trimmed in what looked like walnut.

The cheery woman at the front directed her back to the doctor's private office.

"Dr. Preston?"

"Just one second. Come on in. I need to finish a note on a chart."

CJ sat and watched Clayton's partner scribble words on a paper file. The computer on his desk was turned off. *Old-fashioned guy*, she thought.

Preston himself was round and shiny. His bald head gleamed, his wire-frame glasses caught the light, even his teeth seemed to sparkle. He finished the notes and tossed the paperwork into his out-box. CJ spared a moment of pity for whomever was going to be responsible for transcribing them later.

Preston leaned back in his chair and said, "So you're Clayton's long-lost gay sister. I can see the family resemblance."

It sounded like an automatic opener. She and Clayton never looked a lot alike. It put her on her guard.

"I'm the one," CJ acknowledged. "Although I wasn't so much lost as far, far away."

He laughed forcefully. *Well, aren't you the jolly one?*

"It was nice of you to take the time to see me," CJ said.

"I always have time in a busy day for women who bring me lunch."

She sorted out sandwiches between them, letting him have his pick of the options. He unwrapped his sandwich on his desk and took a hefty bite.

"'s good," he muttered around the bread.

Clearly eating was first on their agenda, so CJ ate her sandwich as well as she could from her lap.

Preston finished first and said, "Be right back."

He left the office and left CJ nonplussed. He was back in five minutes and said, "Sorry. Got to brush and floss right after eating. Patients hate seeing lettuce in their dentist's teeth during the exam."

"I know I would," CJ said.

"So Clayton told me to tell you everything. Let's see, I was born a poor black child in Mississippi…"

He broke up laughing again at his own joke. "Get it? Steve Martin?"

CJ managed a thin smile.

"Oh, I get it," she replied. "*The Jerk*. Very funny."

"The Jerk" indeed, she thought.

"Sorry, sorry." He wiped tears from his eyes. "I always wanted to use that one. So what do you want to know?"

"Have you been having problems in the practice since all this happened?"

Preston grew sober. "Some. Some of our patients have left, a few more have asked to switch to me instead of Clayton. Of course, we've had a few new ones come in, curiosity seekers. One reporter posed as a new patient to try to get an interview. We threw her out, of course."

"Has the practice taken a big financial hit?"

Preston shrugged his shoulders. "Not noticeably. Not yet, anyway. I suppose it depends on how long things take and what the, er, final disposition is."

"So the practice wasn't in financial trouble before all this started?"

"Well, I admit we've had some tough times. But I'm not worried. I have money I inherited from my father. See, I just bought a boat." He grabbed a photograph from his desktop. "It's a Starcraft Fishmaster. Almost twenty-one feet long, two hundred and fifty horsepower. You can get ten people fishing on that sucker."

CJ would have had trouble naming a topic that held less interest for her than fishing boats. She handed the photo back and said, "Very nice. But the word is that Clayton is having serious financial troubles. Is that not true?"

"Oh, it's true, all right," Preston admitted. "He takes his draw first thing each month and has had to have an advance a few times. He's spending every dime he makes and more. I'm betting he's got a boatload of credit card debt. I think his mother had to bail him out when he divorced Paula or he would have had to file bankruptcy."

That was interesting. "Do you have a theory about why that would be?" she asked.

"It's not hard to figure out. The divorce from Amy cost him a lot in the property settlement, maintenance, and child support. I think the property settlement was paid off, but the other checks he had to keep writing every month. Then Paula got a chunk of property settlement that he had to pay off over time to keep the house. And Missy, oh my God."

"They weren't married long," CJ said. "Surely he wouldn't owe her much."

Preston chuckled, nothing keeping his sense of humor dampened for long.

"That's not the problem. The problem is he cheated on her and now she hates his guts. She is costing him a ton in attorney's fees, and not only his own lawyer. Because she's got no money he has to pay her attorney too. And she is fighting him every single inch. She filed a motion for an equal division of their DVD collection, if you can believe that!"

"Do you think Missy is fighting the divorce because she wants him back?"

"Oh, hell no, honey. She really wants to make him suffer."

And there you had it, CJ thought. Missy wasn't emotionally finished with Clayton yet. She might be sleeping with Donny, but her emotions were still tangled up with Clayton. Instead of love she was filled with hurt and anger. Some people moved through that stage quickly; for others it took years. CJ had known a few cases where the anger never stopped.

Paula had gone through whatever animosity she had felt and was at the opposite of love: indifference. Missy was still tangled up in love's wreckage.

She let Preston go back to work and waited in Clayton's office while he finished with his patient. She cleared a few emails from her account and called in to her office, but all seemed well in hand.

When Clayton finally appeared, he was stripping off his latex gloves.

"Sorry, everything always takes longer with a new patient. How'd it go with Pres?"

"He was helpful, in between the bad jokes and me having to admire his boat."

"Oh God, that damn boat. You'd have thought he welded the stupid thing together himself. I know every third person in Savannah fishes, but I don't get the appeal. I mean, I like a nice day out on the river on a sailboat but fishing? I just don't get it."

"I join you in your indifference," CJ said. "He also told me you're up to your neck in debt."

Clayton was silent for a minute. "Yeah, well you probably already knew that. I was partially supporting Amy and Laura, of course, still paying off Paula and this thing with Missy—God, it's been a nightmare."

"You had choices, Clayton. You could have sold the house."

He smiled wryly.

"It wouldn't have helped much. I'm not upside down exactly, but by the time I paid the realtor and cleared the first and second mortgages, plus the line of credit I had on it, the proceeds wouldn't even cover all the money I owe the goddamn lawyers. Mama had to loan me money a couple of years ago, did Preston tell you that? I'd have had to file a Chapter Seven liquidation bankruptcy without it."

Very quietly CJ said, "You could have called me, Clayton."

"Could I? And what would you have said? I can guess. 'Fuck off, Clayton. It's your mess, now clean it up yourself.' That's what."

"I'm here now, aren't I?"

He stared at her across the desk.

"Why are you here, Belle? To watch my life crash and burn? To make Mama happy, because I can tell you nothing we ever do will accomplish that. Because you feel guilty about not coming to Dad's funeral?"

"I'll tell you what I told Alex when she asked me why I was coming. I'm here because whatever else has happened, you're the only brother I have. I couldn't do nothing if there was anything I could do to help. I don't feel guilty, Clayton. I'm trying to make sure I never will."

He slumped over and CJ could see the age in his face clearly for the first time.

"I talked to Tayla this morning," he said. "She stayed over last night and we had dinner with Laura. Tayla wanted to know how you were getting on. She's got some parent meeting tonight, but are you up to meeting us for drinks or something tomorrow?"

"Sure. When?"

They settled on five thirty at Conroy's Pub. CJ wondered if they had her favorite scored flounder on the appetizer menu.

CHAPTER ELEVEN

Alex decided it was time for an experiment. She stopped by Chris Anderson's desk and said, "Do you happen to have lunch plans today? I know Frank said he had to run an errand."

"No, nothing in particular," Chris responded. "You inviting me out, boss?"

"Yes, but I should tell you I have an ulterior motive."

"My favorite kind of lunch." Chris smiled. "Are we going to the deli across the street?"

"Yes, but we're going the long way."

"Huh?"

"I'll explain on the way. Grab your jacket."

They walked downstairs together, chatting about Chris's girlfriend and her new job at St. Anthony's Hospital in the trauma care unit.

"I think she's hooked on the adrenaline rush," Chris said as they pushed out the front doors. "It's like being a cop. Nothing happens for hours and then everything happens at once and it's life or death."

"Yes," Alex agreed. "Though usually no one's shooting at the nurses."

Chris looked grim. "They'd better not. So what exactly are we doing?"

"We are trying," Alex said, "to spot the woman who's been following me, maybe."

"Oh, yeah, Frank might have mentioned something. Beat-up blue Toyota Corolla sedan, right?"

"Yes, I know as the owner of a cherry-red Mustang you're offended by her ride, but that's what we're looking for. Of course, if we leave on foot she may follow on foot. Did you see her driver's license photo?"

"I glanced at it. So we're walking and trying not to be seen looking for her."

"That's pretty much it. For your trouble, I'm buying lunch."

"This keeps getting better and better. Let's go."

They walked down the block, maintaining an earnest conversation. Alex scanned every parked car and every car that passed them on the street in either direction but didn't see the blue Toyota. They continued for another block down the street.

Chris stopped abruptly and bent as if to tie her shoelaces.

"That trick works better if you're not wearing slip-on shoes," Alex pointed out.

"She can't see that from here. A possible, across the street at three o'clock."

Alex tried to make her glance over as casual as she could. The woman was wearing jeans and a light sweater, with a huge handbag over one shoulder. It was hard to get a clear look at her face, but Alex thought she recognized the same limp hairstyle.

"I think that's her," Alex said. "Good catch. Now let's head back. I've worked up an appetite."

"Aren't we going over for a little chat?"

"Nope. If she's following me, I don't want to scare her off until I have some better idea of why she's doing it. Frank's still working on seeing what information he can turn up. Let's see what else we can find out."

"Okay, but I have a request, boss."

"What's that?"

"When you do decide to have your talk with her, let Frank and me ride along, okay? She might look harmless, but not everybody who turns out to be dangerous looks that way. I don't like that she's following my police captain around. Most especially since Lieutenant St. Clair is out of town. Have you told her?"

"There's no point. It would just worry her for no reason and there's nothing she can do about it. Believe me, I'm not crazy about being followed either. I promise not to confront her without help. Now let's get you some corned beef on rye."

"Nice of you to remember."

It was Alex's turn to make the call that night.

"How was your day?" she asked CJ.

"Well, easier than Sunday was, I guess. Though that's not saying much." After a moment of hesitation, she added, "There's something I should have told you about Sunday."

"It was a tough day. I'm not surprised you forgot something."

"I didn't forget. I wanted to give it some thought before we discussed it."

Given the growing list of information that Alex was not telling her partner, she was hardly in a position to condemn.

"It's fine, sweetheart," Alex reassured her. "There's a lot going on. What's up?"

"Laura is afraid that if Clayton goes to prison, she'll have to go live with Mama. Amy doesn't have any family and there's really no one else."

Alex absorbed that information and wondered that they hadn't thought about it before.

"Did you offer?" she asked.

"I would never do that without talking with you, darlin', you know that. No, she asked. But I told her we'd work something out. After I talked to you, of course."

"But you still had to think about it."

"I know we decided not to have children of our own and I'm fine with that decision, I truly am. But this is a major life-changing thing and, yes, I wanted to give it some serious consideration before we talked."

"You know we're Charlie's designated guardians, if anything happens to Nicole."

"I know, but that feels different. Charlie's a little boy and we've both known him a long time and he knows us. If God forbid something happened, there's nothing we wouldn't do for him. Laura's my niece, but we don't know her at all. And it's not like I've been exactly close to my family."

"But she is family," Alex reminded her. "And if the worst happens, we'll figure out what to do. If she has to live here, we will make that work somehow. We will."

"Oh, Alex," CJ murmured, and the next moment Alex could hear a small sob.

"Sweetheart, don't cry, for God's sake," Alex pleaded. "I can't get at you from sixteen hundred miles away."

"I'm sorry. I'm sorry. I'm just tired and frustrated and…"

"And what?"

"This is going to sound foolish."

"You've never sounded foolish in your life. Try me."

"When I'm at home, going through my day, I'm not constantly reminded that I'm a lesbian. I eat breakfast, I go to work, we go to a movie and I'm not constantly thinking, 'But remember, you're different from these other people because you're gay.' I mean, sometimes it's in the forefront, when someone gives us a look or makes a comment. But for the most part it's only one part of who I am. It's not everything I am every minute. Sometimes I'm being a police officer, sometimes I'm being a friend, sometimes I'm just driving down the street, and yes, sometimes I'm your lover. But not every second of the day."

"But not in Georgia."

"Alex, I feel like I'm wearing the scarlet 'L' all the time. Every single person I talk to who knows anything about me feels the need to mention it or wants to know more about it or calls me a name. I know there's a lot of prejudice in the world, I get it. And I know I've been spared some of it because of how I look. But it's starting to make me really angry. And frustrated."

"Frustrated that we still have so far to go."

"Yes, that. And also I'm…frustrated."

Alex listened to her silence for a moment. "As in frustrated, frustrated?"

"Like that. I'm getting all the hateful part of being a lesbian without getting the many benefits."

"Well, I can't change the South in one evening," Alex said, "but I might be able to do something about your lack of benefits."

"And how are you going to do that, darlin', from sixteen hundred miles away?"

"I have skills. Are you in bed?"

"Yes, I'm in bed with a book."

"Then I know what you're not wearing. Put the book on your nightstand."

She heard a sharp intake of breath.

"Are you actually suggesting phone sex to me?" CJ asked.

"And your problem with that would be what, exactly?"

"We've never done that before."

"Was that an objection?"

After a moment CJ said, "No objection. What exactly did you have in mind?"

"I'm thinking if I were there, you know exactly where I would want to touch you. You'll just have to do it for me."

"Alex…"

Dropping her voice low, Alex whispered, "I miss your breasts. Touch them for me."

"Oh. Oh yes, I will."

"So soft. It feels good, doesn't it?"

"Yes."

"Tell me."

"It feels nice."

"Your nipples are hard now, aren't they?"

"Yes." CJ groaned a little.

"Good, that's good. Give them plenty of attention, like I would if I were there."

"God, Alex."

Alex listened to her breathing for a minute.

"Darlin', I want to…"

"Not yet. I'm not finished with your breasts yet. I'm going to use my mouth now. Remember what that feels like?"

"Yes, I remember. I…please, Alex."

"What do you want?" Alex murmured. "Tell me."

"I want…I want you to…Alex, please!"

"All right. Are you sure you're ready? Are you wet for me, sweetheart?"

"God, Alex, yes!"

"Then touch yourself. Wherever you want, like I would. Remember my hand on you, my mouth on you, my fingers inside you."

CJ's breathing grew labored and Alex's imagination treated her to a vivid picture of CJ squirming naked in the sheets. The warmth ran through her own body and she knew CJ wouldn't be the only one self-pleasuring tonight.

She heard a single moan. Alex whispered into the phone, "Come for me, honey."

The cry at the other end signaled the climax she reveled in providing. She listened to CJ's breathing for another couple of minutes, almost as satisfied as if she'd actually brought CJ to orgasm with her body rather than her voice.

"Alex," CJ finally managed to say. "That was…unbelievable. I didn't know y'all could do that."

"You did it," Alex said. "You were ready. I just helped. And it was very good for me."

"Was it? Because I think this phone call isn't over yet."

Alex smiled. Suddenly her clothes seemed very confining.

Nothing quite like a good night's sleep to give you an energetic start the next morning, CJ thought. She had her travel cup of coffee and her notebook at the ready. It was canvassing day.

It took her all morning to talk to every one of Amy's neighbors she could find. Some were gone, of course, but a gratifying number of people were home: the retired, the stay-at-home parents, the telecommuters and freelancers. Many didn't have anything to tell her, but a surprising number knew Amy and were willing to talk about "that nice woman, such a tragedy."

Willingness to talk didn't mean that they had anything to add to CJ's notebook of information. The worst thing anyone had to say about Amy was that she didn't always bring her garbage cans in right away after the trash truck had been by. No one had anything bad to say about Laura either. She was part of the crew of teenagers who did a neighborhood cleanup every fall, helping bag the heaps of leaves the many trees shed.

One neighbor did confirm Laura's story about the mystery man in Amy's life.

"I did hear a car pulling away one night. It was one of those loud, sports-car types."

"When was that, do you remember?" CJ asked.

"It was right after the news came on WSAV, because I said something to Carl about it. Must have been, I'd say a month ago, maybe. It was still real hot, I remember that."

But she couldn't describe whoever had been driving or even the car itself. All it left CJ with was the confirmation that Laura had been telling the truth, which CJ had never seriously doubted in the first place.

She'd run out of coffee and the return of the humid September heat left her in need of a bathroom, a rest and a cold drink. She found a diner nearby and decided to put her break to good use.

It was time for her to review what she knew so far. The evidence hadn't changed significantly since her initial review on the airplane flight to Savannah. The prosecution had Clayton's motive, his lack of an alibi, the gun found in his car and the jacket. His defense team had his lack of animosity for Amy, the lack of a confession and the negative gunshot residue test, which was not much. All she'd done was to confirm that Clayton needed money and verify that the shooter wore gloves, making the negative findings on the GSR test irrelevant and damaging Clayton's case further. The negative GSR test on the hoodie was still a point in his favor, but it clearly hadn't stopped the Savannah police from arresting him.

So how much progress had she made in finding another viable suspect?

Leading the field by a full length was Missy. Her hatred for Clayton was unconcealed. She would have had to have Donny's help, so their mutual alibi didn't mean much. CJ needed to think about how she might determine any other ties they might have had to the gun, the jacket or the place and time of Amy's murder.

Paula looked to be a longshot at best. It would have been physically difficult for her to have done the murder herself given the time constraints of her alibi. She could have hired someone, CJ supposed, but what was her motive? Clayton had almost finished paying off her property settlement, and any feelings Paula might have had for him seemed to have died long ago. CJ made a note to contact the real estate client Paula had been with that night on Tybee Island, but she wasn't optimistic that the lead would help her case.

The wild card was someone she hadn't met yet: Tayla's husband. If he resented Clayton sleeping with his wife, that gave him a good motive. Again, CJ had to wonder: why would he go to the trouble of killing Amy to frame Clayton instead of taking the direct route and shooting Clayton himself?

In fact, why wouldn't Missy have done that as well? Why shoot Amy if Clayton was the real target? But if the purpose was to kill Amy all along, then why bother to frame Clayton or anyone else? Framing someone for a crime was popular in fiction, but rarely happened in reality, in CJ's experience. Would Amy's mystery beau even know enough about Clayton to be able to frame him?

It didn't make sense to her. She was missing something, somewhere.

Maybe Mama told Charles the butler to shoot her ex-daughter-in-law so Clayton's money troubles would be resolved. That theory made about as much sense as anything else CJ had come up with so far.

Her energy from the morning had drained away. She finished her tea. It was time for a nap back at the hotel. She had drinks with Clayton and Tayla tonight, and she had nothing particularly good to report to them.

Alex finished washing her hands and as she exited the women's room, she almost ran Chris Anderson down.

"Sorry," Chris said. "Frank sent me to look for you."

"What's going on?" Alex asked.

"We have an update for you on the mysterious Ms. Goetz." Frank was already sitting in Alex's office.

"Hey, Cap," he greeted her. "Heard you and my partner had an interesting lunch last week."

Alex sat behind her desk and looked at the notes in Frank's hands.

"The lunch was fine, but it was the walk beforehand that made it fun. What have you found out?"

He consulted his paperwork. "We've looked everywhere we can think of," he began. "You never arrested anybody named Goetz that we can find, and I can't trace any connection to anybody else interesting, like somebody who just got out on parole." He hesitated and Chris jumped in.

"We also checked out the woman you shot last year. I wanted to make sure she was safely buttoned up in the State Hospital in Pueblo because she's still several french fries short of a Happy Meal."

Frank guffawed. "Where the hell did you come up with that one? A Happy Meal?"

Chris lifted blond eyebrows at him.

"A brick short of a load? Half a bubble off plumb? One card shy of a full deck? One crayon short of…"

"Stop! You're killing me here," Frank said.

"Well, anyway, she's still crazy and she's still locked up," Chris concluded.

Alex looked thoughtfully at Frank. He often seemed hesitant to bring up sensitive topics with her. She worried about the effect his reluctance might have if he were promoted. Certainly dealing with command level staff and managing officers required tact, but he also needed the mental fortitude to deliver the hard news on occasion, regardless of consequences. Would Frank be able to do that? Alex tucked the question back into her mind to ruminate over later.

"All right," Alex said. "Anybody on the squad working on anything now that might be a connection?"

Both detectives shook their heads.

"We asked around," Frank said. "Nobody had an idea. We've got a big fat nothing."

Alex sighed. "Okay. What else do you know about Ms. Goetz?"

Frank consulted his notes again.

"Not much," he conceded. "She's living in the house on Webster. It's a rental and she's got a live-in boyfriend. There were four calls to Denver PD on domestic stuff in the last two years, complaints from the neighbors about yelling and throwing things. No indication that he hits her, though, so no arrests."

"Does the boyfriend have a sheet?"

"Not for domestic violence. Three arrests for assault and battery, bar fight kinda stuff. Oh, and one municipal arrest for my favorite offense."

Chris smirked.

"Public urination," she announced. "He hates that."

Frank made a face. "Well, it's just gross."

Chris laughed at him.

"The guy will wade into a shotgun homicide crime scene with no problem, but one dude peeing on a building and he gets all squirrelly on me."

Alex said, "You know how much I truly enjoy the comedy stylings of Morelli and Anderson, but is there any chance you could finish giving me this report?"

"Anyway," Frank resumed, "she works shifts at the Pancake Palace on South Broadway. Mornings mostly, which could explain how she was free to follow you around in the middle or end of the day."

Alex fixed him with a look. "And unless you've already spooked her by going in and asking her manager about her, how the hell would you have that information?"

"Um. Well…" Frank looked at the ceiling for inspiration.

Chris jumped into the conversation again.

"There may have been a bit of surveillance last weekend. You know, the sitting in the car stuff," she added.

Alex said sternly, "No more of that, am I completely clear? And don't give me the 'We were off-duty' line either. Do not follow her, surveille her, contact her or anything else. Any questions about those instructions?"

"No, Cap."

"Got it, boss," Chris added.

"Good. It looks to me like there is no good reason on earth why this woman should be following me around periodically, so I can only think of one more thing to do."

"What's that?" Frank said, getting out his pen.

"You don't have to write it down," Alex said.

"What are you going to do?"

"I'm going to ask her."

Frank exchanged a look with Chris.

"Ah, Lieutenant St. Clair is still out of town, right?" he asked.

"I've already discussed this with your partner," Alex said.

"She promised to let us come with her," Chris interjected.

"That's not exactly what I said," Alex pointed out dryly. "But since you two have a hard time walking the straight and narrow, you will be coming." She lifted a hand to forestall questions. "At a time and day of my choosing and under the conditions I set up, all right? Until then you will drop this entirely and you will not go anywhere near her. All clear on that?"

"Got it, Cap," Frank said, looking relieved.

"But don't go without us," Chris added. "This woman might be a taco short of a combination plate."

Frank groaned.

Conroy's Pub was less jam-packed than it had been at lunch the week before when CJ met with Paula. Today she arrived at almost the same moment as Clayton and Tayla and they agreed to wait while a river view table became available.

To make an easier connection, CJ said, "I don't think I've ever heard of anyone named Tayla before. Is it a family name?"

"Hardly," Tayla answered. "My parents made it up. They were at a soccer game and some parent who was from Boston or New England or somewhere like that was calling their kid. The kid was named Taylor, of course, but he kept yelling "Tayla!" They thought it was cute, so that's how I ended up as the only Tayla anyone's ever heard of."

CJ smiled. "It's good to have a story like that."

Tayla eyed her. "What's yours? What does 'CJ' stand for?"

"Not one but two family names. Christabelle Johnson. The Johnson is from an ancestor who was a Civil War hero."

"Which side?"

Clayton laughed. "Honey, believe me. We're not allowed to have any Yankee ancestors. The guy once took a Union armory without firing a shot by assembling a bunch of fake cannons out of stovepipes. That's why they called him 'Stovepipe' Johnson. Lost his eyesight in the war and still managed to raise six kids."

"Did you play soccer growing up?" CJ asked Tayla.

"No. It bores me to death. You run for an hour and a half and score maybe once. Basketball was my sport." She eyed CJ. "Did you play?"

"Neither basketball or soccer. Tennis was my favorite. I still play occasionally."

They sat at their table. The sun's lowering rays caught the river's silver stream, dancing in bright steps along the surface. CJ sighed happily. One thing she certainly missed about Savannah was the sense of being surrounded by the water, rivers and bays and the ocean beyond. It was good to be back here for a little while. She began to plan another visit sometime. She really wanted Alex to see where she grew up and for them to enjoy the unique beauty and history of Savannah together. Now perhaps Alex could meet Clayton and Laura and…

"Belle, what are we doing here? Appetizers, like that?"

Tayla said, "Yes dear, we can share the apps, but God, I need a drink. Or three. Every day with those kids is like being trapped in a fun house and the semester just started."

CJ wondered how to introduce the topic of Tayla's ex-husband, but she continued her fascination with Tayla's distaste for her job. She asked, "Did you study elementary education at college?"

Tayla barked a laugh.

"Hell no. I studied art. I had to get my teaching certificate after I moved to Georgia because it turned out that Ray was incapable of holding a job for longer than seventeen minutes."

Clayton said, "She's a great painter. She did the piece in my house, the seascape in the living room."

"Yes, I remember. It was lovely."

CJ did recall the painting with all the wrong colors for the room. She switched back to the topic she really wanted to pursue.

"What does your ex-husband do?"

"I wish he were my ex, but the final decree isn't done yet. Anyway, he's a salesman or so he claims. Cars, computers, appliances, whatever he can get."

"Is he working now?"

"I believe he's currently trying to sell electronics at Southern Technologies on Abercorn. He's had the job a couple of months, which may be a new record for him."

Clayton gave CJ a look of disapproval. CJ read it as "quit talking about her ex-husband." She had what she wanted to know so she asked smoothly, "Tell me more about your painting, Tayla. What medium do you like best?"

The drinks arrived and everyone managed to pretend for a while that they were a normal group, the sister meeting the new girlfriend. The appetizers came out of the kitchen eventually: fried green tomatoes, crab cakes, and jalapeno corn bread. The corn bread came with Vidalia onion jam and it was so good CJ barely managed to keep from eating it all herself with a spoon.

"How's Laura doing?" she asked Clayton.

He shrugged. "Okay, I guess. Some days she seems normal. Other days she's like a little kid and then she'll get bitchy for no reason."

Tayla reached over and patted his hand. "She'll be fine, honey. You should really try the crab cake. The aioli is fabulous."

After Tayla finished her second Tom Collins, she poked Clayton in the ribs.

"Let me out, honey. I have to go to the ladies' room."

He slid out of his seat and she swung her purse onto her shoulder as she crossed the room. He watched her go and CJ could appreciate why: the woman did have a nice rear view.

He turned back to her and said, "You want to tell me what all that was about?"

"Which part?"

"Don't be funny, Belle. What's with all the questions about her ex-husband?"

"Clayton, this is what investigators do. Contrary to what you see on television, we go from place to place and ask people questions. Then we go away and think about things and we go back and ask more questions. No kicking in doors, no gunfights in the street, just information gathering."

"I understand, but what the hell does Ray Morrison have to do with anything?"

"Clayton, you're sleeping with his wife. In my line of work, that's called a motive."

"That's ridiculous. He might come after me, but he'd never hurt Amy. No one would hurt Amy."

CJ shook her head.

"I spent all morning talking to her neighbors. I've talked to her employer. And I agree with you, everyone liked Amy. No one would hurt her. And yet she's dead, Clayton. Someone lay in wait for her and deliberately shot her to death. So somebody did want to hurt her."

To her shock, Clayton's blue eyes blurred over with tears. He knuckled them angrily away.

"Goddammit, Belle! I know that. But I don't understand anything else that's going on!"

CJ reached across the table to grip his arm tightly. "I'm sorry, Clayton. I'm not trying to hurt you. But if I'm going be of any help to you at all, you have to let me do my work. Sometimes people get angry or annoyed with me, but it goes with the job. Let me do what I came here to do."

The next day dawned in a gray haze. As CJ dressed, she decided that calling Ray Morrison before the interview wasn't her best move. Some interviews went better when people were surprised by them. Of course, that worked better when she showed up with some official authority. She decided her best bet was to take the same approach that had worked for her, more or less, with Missy. She'd give Ray a chance to have an audience for all of his grievances against Clayton.

She hoped the sympathetic ear approach would work.

Traffic down Abercorn was almost as bad as Colorado Boulevard back in Denver. CJ wasn't in a hurry. She wanted time for Ray Morrison to be settled into work without waiting so long that he got too busy to talk to her.

Southern Electronics was a typical big box electronics and appliance retailer. The large parking lot was almost empty when CJ pulled in. The store had only been open half an hour, so she was pleased with her timing.

As she got out of the rental car, she shifted her weapon a little back on her hip. She was wearing a linen blazer to cover it. This was the first day she'd worn it outside, but she remembered Tayla saying her husband was a "gun nut," and after Alex's warning, she decided to be cautious. Her normal service weapon was a Sig Sauer semiautomatic, but she hadn't brought it on this trip. Her backup gun was a much smaller Smith & Wesson .38 caliber five-shot revolver. It was simple to conceal and not very heavy. It had been worth checking a bag at the airport so that she could bring it with her.

She strolled into the store and wandered up and down the rows of cell phones, game consoles and a dizzying array of television sets. Several employees offered to help her find what she was looking for, but she declined politely. The employees conveniently had their first names on their shirts, so she figured all she had to do was wait for the right one to show up.

It took a long time. She'd been wandering almost an hour. There had been a brief text exchange with Alex over the type of game system their nephew owned: she could never remember, whether it was Nintendo or Xbox. She picked up a game she thought he might like and was playing with the new cell phones when a middle-aged man in the store's bright yellow polo shirt appeared.

"Can I help you?"

His shirt had "Ray" embroidered on his left chest. He seemed to be about Tayla's age, with dark hair receding dramatically from his temples. He also smelled of stale cigarette smoke, which she thought might explain where he'd been for so long.

CJ gave him a bright smile and said, "Ray Morrison?"

To her surprise he lifted his hands and began backing away from her.

"Whatever the hell papers you're trying to serve me with, I'm not taking them!"

CJ showed her own hands, empty of anything except a new video game from Disney.

"I'm not a process server, I promise. I just want to ask you a couple of questions."

"Did she send you? The bitch I was married to?"

"No. She doesn't know I'm here."

He dropped his hands but continued to look at her suspiciously.

"Yeah? So who the hell are you, then?"

"My name is CJ St. Clair. I'm Clayton St. Clair's sister and I'm here to ask you about his ex-wife's murder."

"Fuck off!"

A couple of customers glanced their direction. CJ reassured them with a sunny smile and continued in a low tone, "Let's walk a bit. I will be so interested in the newest cell phones and you can tell me what a son-of-a-bitch my brother is."

She strolled down the display case and then stopped, waiting for him to join her.

He finally stepped next to her. "Lady, what the hell do you want from me? Your brother is screwing my wife and she's screwing me, but not the same way. What the fuck business is it of yours?"

"I'm trying to figure out if he really killed his ex-wife or not." Well, that was one way of putting it, she supposed, the way that would be most palatable to Ray Morrison.

He grunted expressively.

"He probably did. And my wife probably put him up to it."

"Why would you say that?"

"Look, I'm sure you know all about your brother's zipper, the one he can't keep zipped up. That fucker's gotta have at least two women at the same time or he ain't having any fun. What you don't know is how much shit my wife can do to a guy's head."

This had taken an interesting direction. "Tell me all about it."

Morrison grunted again and gave her a side-eye expression. "You really want hear all this crap?"

"I do, actually," CJ said.

"Well, you're gonna get the short story version because I can't afford to lose this job. The thing is…have you met Tayla?"

"Yes. Twice."

"And I bet she told you what a screwup I am, can't keep a job?"

"Something like that."

"Well, here's what she does. I get a sales job, see? And then she does whatever she can to get me canned. She calls my boss with some crap, or she takes my car and hides her keys so I can't get to work, all kinds of shit. The only reason I'm still on this job is I told my manager what she'd pulled in the past. He understood, he had a bitch ex-wife too, so when she called him he told her to take a hike. Pissed her off real good."

CJ flipped a mental coin. Was Ray suffering from paranoid delusions? Or was Tayla a master manipulator?

"Why would she do that?" she asked.

This time the grunt came out as half a sigh.

"I've been trying to figure that out since the day I married her. God knows she loves yelling at me when I get fired, maybe it gets her rocks off or something. She keeps telling me sales isn't a 'real job' and that I should be working in a bank or something making more money. But hell, I like sales, talking to people and finding stuff they need. It's not like we were on welfare. She was never happy, not for one minute."

CJ digested this information. Another employee passed by, and Ray launched into a discussion of iPhone versus Android until she was out of earshot.

"I'm sorry I can't help you," Ray said. "But I know Tayla. She uses other people to get what she wants. If I had to guess, I think your brother probably did shoot his ex because Tayla wanted the money they said in the paper he was going to get. That's really her style."

"Where were you the night Amy was killed?" she asked him.

She waited for another explosion of temper, but he shook his head.

"At home by myself watching the Braves game on television. And no, I can't prove it. I told the cops that and they haven't been back since."

"Do you hate Clayton for having an affair with your wife?"

He looked at her directly. "Yeah, I do. I think he's a shithead. But he's gonna get his. Because Tayla will screw him over six ways to Sunday. And if he did kill somebody because she told him to, she's got her hooks in him so deep he'll never get any peace this side of the grave."

CHAPTER TWELVE

CJ's brain was tired. She had a list of phone calls to make and she decided she'd had enough of driving all over town. The calls could just as easily be made from her hotel room where she could take her gun off and wear her sweatpants.

Her frustration was mounting. In a week's solid work she had almost nothing concrete to give to Clayton's attorney. She'd met her niece and made a start at getting to know who she was. She and Clayton were beginning to forge a friendship of sorts, albeit a tenuous one. And she discovered Alex was as sexy over the phone as CJ found her in person. She smiled at the memory.

As she drove down Abercorn she spotted a huge bookstore in a mall with a large parking structure. On impulse she made a turn into the garage. She was almost finished with the book she'd brought and thought she might want to pick up another one. Alex had gotten her an e-reader last Christmas, but CJ just hadn't been able to give up reading real paper, flipping back and forth as she pleased.

She spent a pleasant hour in the bookstore browsing the shelves. A new collection called *Poets of the New South* caught her eye and she found another book as well. She got a coffee on the way out to her car and was feeling refreshed already.

The remote door opener on the rental car keychain chirped as CJ hit the button to unlock her car.

The next sound she heard was an ear-shattering bang.

Gunshot.

The windshield of her car spider-webbed and she heard the sound of broken glass through the ringing in her ears. She screamed, "Get down! Sniper!" at the top of her lungs, and she dropped into an immediate crouch beside her front tire.

CJ didn't remember dropping the book bag or reaching for her gun, but the revolver was in her hand. Someone far away screamed, the sound echoing through the garage, but it sounded like fear rather than a person who was injured.

"Stay down! Everybody stay down!"

A second shot shattered the passenger side window and CJ hit the ground. The sound of her heart pounding in her ears made it hard to listen for footsteps. She took a glance under the car searching for anyone approaching on foot.

Nothing.

A slamming car door was the next sound she heard. Where was it?

The echo from the concrete walls made it hard to determine the direction. She resumed her crouch, searching with her eyes for any movement.

A pickup truck roared away from her, racing down the aisle.

The temptation to put some bullets into the cab nearly overwhelmed CJ, but she brought the revolver down. There was no way to be completely certain that the driver was the one who'd shot at her and even if she could be sure, her .38 caliber bullets might ricochet from the truck or one of the concrete pillars. She couldn't risk a shot going wild.

"God damn it all to hell!" she exclaimed.

She fumbled for her cell phone. "Is anybody hurt? Anyone?"

A couple of muffled voices replied, "Okay! We're all right!"

"Y'all stay put," CJ instructed. "The police will be here in a minute."

Detective Tyson Monroe was the best-dressed plainclothes cop CJ had ever met. He was a slim African-American man probably in his early thirties, and he looked sharp, from his short hair to his immaculate thin mustache to the polish on his oxfords.

As the paramedic finished bandaging the palm of her hand, CJ wondered if he had family money, a rich wife or spent every dime of his disposable income on clothes.

He finished talking to the last witness and came toward her, tugging down his shirt cuff slightly. He was wearing actual honest-to-God cufflinks.

"Miz St. Clair," he greeted her. "How's the hand?"

She displayed her right hand and its small patch of gauze.

"I just scraped it when I hit the concrete. It stings, but I think I'm going to live. Fortunately I'm left-handed, so I'll be able to brush my teeth tonight."

He pursed his lips. *Not a big sense of humor*, CJ suspected.

"I've heard from everyone else," he said. "You want to tell me your version?"

His tone of voice irritated her, but CJ kept her response mild and factual. Yes, a white pickup with a Georgia plate. No, she didn't see a license plate number. No, she couldn't give him a more precise description of the vehicle that she seen racing away from her for about a second and a half. And no, she didn't see who had taken the gunshots at her.

"You seem pretty certain that they were shooting at you," Monroe said.

"I assume you'll examine the car," CJ said dryly. "I was about to get in it when the first bullet went through the windshield. Looks like a pretty powerful handgun, nine millimeter or maybe a .357. It left a hole the size of a quarter and I'm sure you'll find the slug somewhere in the driver's seat. The passenger window was shattered, so I assume whoever it was changed his angle of fire when he saw me duck down."

Monroe looked thoughtful. "So if he'd waited about thirty more seconds he'd have gotten you, you're thinking."

CJ shuddered involuntarily. She'd been shot once in her life and that had been more than enough for her.

"Yes," she agreed with him. "But I don't think he was impatient."

"You don't?" He sounded skeptical.

"No, I don't. For the bullet to go through the glass like that he had to be fairly close, just a few feet away. It's possible to miss twice from that distance, but I think whoever did this was a better shot than that."

Monroe gazed for a moment at the crime scene technicians working on her car and the uniformed officers on the scene.

"And I'm here because you think this is connected to your brother's case," he said flatly.

CJ said, "Well, I doubt if this is a random shooting and so do you. Assuming I was targeted, I can't think of another reason for someone to take a couple of shots at me. Unless they're antiliteracy and they hate women who buy books."

He returned his dark gaze to her and she sighed. No sense of humor at all.

"So your theory is that someone among all these people you've been going around and talking to while you've been messing around in my case, someone of those other people murdered Amy St. Clair and now they're trying to warn you off, is that it?"

"I can't think of a better theory right offhand. Can you, Detective?"

"I've got one."

"Want to share?"

"Sure. You staged this to draw attention away from your brother and set up this very possibility in my mind. I'm sure your brother's high-end lawyer will try to get this incident before the jury to prove that very theory."

"Seriously? I'm a police officer, Detective."

"Yeah, well even cops have families. And you'd know how to set this up to look good, wouldn't you?"

She handed over her revolver. "Check it. It hasn't been fired. All the bullets are there and you won't find any in my car."

He glanced at the gun and opened the cylinder briefly before handing it back.

"I didn't say you fired the shots. I'm sure you had a willing accomplice to haul ass out of here in a truck for the benefit of the witnesses."

This was getting ridiculous from CJ's perspective.

"How did I find this helpful coconspirator? Angie's List?"

"Let's just say I'll be checking on where your brother was this afternoon."

"Oh, my goodness, Detective. Well, while you're at it you might want to check out a few other people. Like Melissa, my brother's current wife, and her boyfriend. Or Ray Morrison, whom I left no more than a couple of hours ago. Or…"

"I can complete my investigation into this shooting without your help, Miz St. Clair. And I'd appreciate it if you'd stop screwing around with this case. If you're right and somebody is actually trying to warn you off, the best way to prevent a repeat incident is to stop doing it." He handed her a card. "I'm assuming you will be cooperating fully with the Savannah Chatham Metropolitan Police Department in this investigation. If you should have any further information, please don't hesitate to call me."

He walked off toward the rental car. CJ wanted nothing more than to leave immediately, but she had no way back to the hotel until the rental car agency showed up with her replacement vehicle.

She'd spilled her coffee when she dove for the pavement. She decided she'd treat herself to another one inside the bookstore while she called her insurance company.

It was after three when she made it back to her hotel. If the valet thought it was odd that she'd left in a gray luxury sedan and returned in a red one, he didn't comment.

When she got to her room, she shrugged off her jacket. Her palm was still stinging and she went in search of some ibuprofen. Then she saw the message light on her bedside phone was blinking red.

She grabbed a water glass and swallowed the pills before she picked up the message.

There was a package downstairs for Miss St. Clair.

Could Alex have sent something? CJ put her jacket back on and went down to the front desk.

The reception clerk handed her a flat brown mailing envelope. All that was typewritten on it was "C J St. Clair."

CJ frowned at it. "How did this arrive?"

"I'm sorry, I don't know. It was on the desk when I came on, and so we left a message for you."

"Do you happen to have any gloves back there? And a baggie, maybe, large enough to put this envelope in?"

"Gloves?"

"Any kind. Maybe the housekeeping staff uses them?"

He was gone for a couple of minutes. CJ let the envelope lie on the marble topped reception desk without touching it.

The clerk returned with a pair of light blue latex gloves and one of the empty plastic bags they used to line the ice buckets. It didn't have a seal on it, but it would do. CJ slipped the gloves on a little awkwardly over her bandaged hand before she picked up the envelope.

It was too flat to contain a bomb, so she pulled open the flap carefully. Inside was a single sheet of white paper.

She turned it over. It said: "I shoot to kill next time, dyke. Leave town now."

She put the envelope and the piece of paper carefully into the plastic bag and asked for some scotch tape to seal it shut. Then she stripped off the gloves and took out her cell phone and the business card that Detective Monroe had given her.

"Detective? You asked me to call you with any further information. I believe I have some items that qualify."

CJ's cell phone rang while she was having dinner in her room.

"Miz St. Clair? Detective Monroe."

"Nice to hear from you, Detective," she said, putting down her fork. "I'm guessing you have news."

"This is a courtesy call," he said. "Because you're a fellow officer. I wouldn't normally be calling a civilian."

He's trying to be nice, CJ thought. *Making an effort.*

"And I appreciate it, Detective. What have you found out?"

"Not much. The slugs in your car were from a .45 caliber semi, not a known gun. The parking garage didn't have a security camera working that day, so no further information on the pickup truck."

CJ sighed. "And any luck on the envelope and note?"

"Prints from the reception desk clerk and one other unidentified person. Might be the person who left it, but more likely someone else who handled it while putting it away. No one saw anybody suspicious in the lobby that morning."

It would be so much easier, CJ reflected, if the bad guys would accommodate us by wearing black trench coats and slinking around.

"I do have one piece of good news," Monroe added.

"We could use some. What would that be?"

"Your brother was with patients at his office all day. He didn't leave, not even for lunch, according to everyone who works there. So it looks like he's off the hook. For today, anyway."

"That is good news."

"You know that doesn't change the fact that he killed his ex-wife."

Was Monroe trying to provoke her? Or was he simply trying to gauge her reaction?

"When I started digging into this case," CJ said carefully, "I tried to approach it the same way I would any case. The question of whether Clayton was guilty or not was still an open one, one I was going to try to answer. I didn't assume he did it. I didn't assume otherwise. You know as well as I do that lack of objectivity leads to bad results."

"I don't see how you could think you could be objective about your own brother."

"I hadn't seen or spoken to my brother for fourteen years before last week. We weren't exactly close buddies. If he killed Amy, I want him in prison, brother or not. But after working on this case for a week, I'm not convinced. But I will say this: if I'd been in your position, I'd have thought he did it too."

"Is that so? Then I have to ask you, professional to professional, why you're not convinced he did it."

"Because his motive is shaky. Our mother has money, I have money. If he needed it that badly, he would have come to us before he thought to kill Amy. And because he's never confessed. In the last week, I've heard various people refer to him as a bastard, a prick and a shithead, and certainly where his personal life is concerned, he's all of those things. But by and large he admits to them. When he screws up, he usually admits it."

She rubbed at the scar on her knee, remembering being shoved off the swing. Clayton had come into the kitchen a few minutes later to give her flowers and apologize.

The apology would have been more effective if he hadn't broken off some of Mama's best irises from her garden. And if he hadn't been lured in by the scent of freshly baked chocolate chip cookies.

"You know as well as I do that not everyone confesses," Monroe said.

"Yes. And you know as well as I do that it's still a point in his favor."

Monroe said, "We're not to resolve this by arguing about it. There will be a jury for that later. Meantime, I suggest you go back to your day job and get out of the heat. Somebody wants you out of the picture."

"Which is a very good reason for me to stay around, I think," CJ replied.

CJ braced herself for the phone call to Alex that night.

"That's it," Alex said in a voice of thunder. "I'm coming out there, no argument."

"No, you're not. Listen to me, darlin'. No one was trying to hurt me. They're trying to warn me off, that's all."

"They fired a gun at you! Twice. I'm coming out."

"Listen to me, Alex. I'm on my guard now. I promise to carry my gun every second I set foot out of the hotel, limit my evening activities and keep an eye out. Oh, and I promise to stay out of parking garages. Which, if I remember correctly, are dangerous places for us."

"Don't joke about this, sweetheart. Do not take this lightly, or I swear to God I'm on the airplane tomorrow."

"I'll be fine," CJ said in her best soothing voice. "I've done enough damage to the Gold Card this month. You stay there and I promise I'll text you hourly, if you want me to. I'm a big girl. Okay?"

"I don't like it," Alex grumbled.

"I know, darlin'. But if my being here is stirring the pot, that could be very good news for Clayton."

"Maybe," Alex conceded. "But I'm more interested in you being safe than your brother getting acquitted."

"I'm going to try very hard to accomplish both."

CHAPTER THIRTEEN

The Pancake Palace on South Broadway in Denver had occupied the same one- story building for more than sixty years. Buildings on both sides had been torn down and renovated: one an office building, the other an upscale design center. But the Palace remained largely untouched by time. The vertical neon sign dated from the nineteen fifties and featured a smiling waitress holding up a tray on which a giant stack of pancakes seemed ready to topple from the plate. The place was open twenty-four hours, and Alex knew it was a favorite of Denver cops. She'd eaten there herself once or twice. If memory served, the tile was cracked in spots and some of the booths had tears in the plastic upholstery, but the coffee was excellent.

She let Chris and Frank go in first and do a quick survey, less because she needed for them to do it and more because they seemed to want to do it. When she came in, she saw they'd taken two seats near the kitchen entrance to cover the rear entrance.

Alex almost smiled. Did they actually think the woman was going to take off and run?

She made eye contact with Frank, and he glanced meaningfully at the man at the cash register and gave her a slight nod. There were only a few other tables with customers, a couple near the front door and three single men at their own tables.

Alex took a booth well away from everyone else. In a couple of minutes Shaylynn Goetz approached her and said, "Would you like a…"

She stopped, the plastic menu in her hand hovering above the tabletop as she gazed at Alex. For a moment Alex thought she had been wrong and that Shaylynn was going to turn and run for the doorway.

Alex said, "I don't need a menu. Sit down, will you? It's okay, we've already talked to the manager. You can take a couple of minutes."

"Wha—what are you doing here? I mean, do I know you?"

Gently Alex said, "Let's not do it that way. Here, sit down, you're so pale I'm afraid you're going to faint."

She slumped into the booth across from Alex. Her face was drained of all color and her eyes were hooded. The dark circles under her eyes stood out as if the flesh were bruised. The woman seemed no more than a stick underneath her polyester uniform. She was so thin Alex automatically checked her arms for needle tracks but saw none.

But she did see real bruising, the clear, fading yellow-green colors spaced evenly against the white skin of her arm. She also spotted a faint discoloration near her jawline.

Apparently Shaylynn had been lying to the Denver PD when she told them her boyfriend didn't hit her.

Shaylynn stuttered, "I…I don't know…you."

Alex said again, "Don't let's waste our time on that part. You know I'm a police officer. I know you've followed me at least three times in the last week. I saw you and I saw your car."

Shaylynn's dark eyes widened.

"You're…you going to arrest me?"

"Not unless you've done something illegal or do something foolish now. And I will tell you there are other police officers in the room in case you do. So just take a deep breath and tell me why you were following me."

The breath was more of a gulp of air than calming breath. Shaylynn leaned her head forward, her chin almost falling between the collarbones that stuck out sharply against her chest. She'd pulled her thin hair back into a ponytail, but one brown lock had escaped and fell over her forehead.

"Do you want help, is that it?" Alex said. "Because I can see where he's hit you, where he's grabbed you. You can come with us right now. File a complaint and we'll get an arrest warrant for him. We can help you find a safe place to go, if that's what you need. You don't have to live with someone who hurts you. No one deserves that."

Her voice in response was barely a whisper. "I do."

"No, you don't," Alex responded firmly. "And until you realize that he's going to keep hurting you."

She shook her head. "You don't understand. If you did, you'd hate me."

"I didn't come here to judge you and I'm not going to hate you. I only want to know why you were following me."

Shaylynn lifted her head a little but still couldn't quite meet Alex's gaze.

"I…I just wanted to know…know more about you. What kind of person you are. Before…before I had to come…and see you. I don't know if…I'm ready yet."

Alex sat quietly for a moment, trying to give her room.

"I'm here now," she said eventually. "So it's time for whatever you have to say to me."

As she waited, she tried to determine what Shaylynn was trying to tell her. Her imagination was insufficient to the task. But even had it been working, she would still never have imagined Shaylynn's next words.

"I…I killed your father."

Shaylynn finished shredding the last bit of the napkins she'd brought when she got Alex coffee. The coffee was freshly brewed and as good as Alex remembered, but today she could hardly taste it as Shaylynn completed her story.

"When I joined AA a few years back," Shaylynn said, "they give you these steps to work on so you can stay sober. You have to take a good hard look at yourself and admit everything you've done wrong in your life. And you're supposed to make it up to people where you can. I…I knew I could never make it up to the man I hit and I didn't want to think about what I'd done to anybody else. I read in the paper after…the next day, that he had two kids. I felt so awful. And I tried to forget about it. But then last week somebody left the Colfax paper on the table after eating and I picked it up.

"And it all came back to me. The story about the fallen officers' memorial and the story about your dad and…and there you were, there was a picture of you and you were a real person. Then I couldn't stop thinking about you. And what I'd done to you. I…"

She'd been fighting tears for the last fifteen minutes and now she surrendered to them. Alex located a crumpled but clean tissue from her bag and handed it to her.

Alex let her cry. She hadn't wept for Charles Ryan for a long time, but she remembered those first months after he died, how utterly alone she had felt. The responsibility of the world felt draped on her shoulders, with Nicole to look after. She'd missed her father every day, every hour it seemed for a long time.

When was the first day she had awakened and not felt like an orphan anymore? She couldn't remember. In hindsight she was sure that her early unsuccessful marriage was due in large part to the aching loneliness she'd felt after her parents were both gone.

Was Shaylynn to blame for all of that? Alex knew her pain was her own. It never worked to lay your grief onto someone else. It looked to her as though Shaylynn had plenty of her own anguish to deal with now.

A man shoved the door open and jerked his head around the room, looking for someone. When he spotted Shaylynn, he was already on his way over to her. Alex got to her feet quickly.

"What the fuck do you think you're doing, Shay?" he yelled. "Talking to the cops about my business?"

Shaylynn faced him, her hands shaking. "Jonny, no. It's nothing to do with you."

He grabbed her hard and twisted her forearm. His fingers closed right over the old bruises Alex had seen before.

Shaylynn cried out.

Alex said, "Let her go right now."

He twisted harder. "Yeah? You're a cop and you're gonna make me?"

"I *am* a cop," Alex said. "And if we have to make you let her go, I promise you won't like it. Now do it!"

"Who the fuck..." he began.

As if by magic Frank and Chris appeared on either side of him.

"Colfax PD," Chris announced.

"Relax, pal," Frank said. "And follow instructions."

Jonny shoved Shaylynn as hard as he could. She fell into Alex. Alex grabbed her to keep her from falling and dragged her a couple of steps back out of his range.

By the time she had Shaylynn steadied on her feet, she looked over to see Jonny lying facedown on the cracked tile. He was squirming under the firm constrictions of Frank's knee in his back and Chris snapping on handcuffs.

They dragged him to his feet and he continued to harangue Shaylynn.

"What did you tell them? What did you say, goddammit!"

"You know what, Jonny? I didn't say a damn thing about your side business in stealing auto parts and working at a chop shop. Oh, oops. I guess they know now."

Chris looked over at Frank.

"We are so getting a Christmas card from Denver PD this year. C'mon, buddy, let's wait outside for your ride to Smith Road. It's a little crowded out there, I hear, but I'm sure you'll manage somehow."

Alex walked over to the manager and asked, "Did you call him?"

"Hey, he's a friend and I thought Shay might need help or something," he said defensively.

Alex looked at him carefully. "I wouldn't want to hear that Shaylynn had any trouble here because of this."

"Uh. No. No trouble."

"That was the right answer."

She returned to Shaylynn and handed her a business card after scribbling on it.

"He won't bond out before tomorrow, I'm guessing," Alex said. "If you need a place to stay, call this number."

Shaylynn looked at the card and lifted her chin. She seemed to be a stronger woman than the one Alex had met a few minutes ago.

"I won't," she answered. "My name is on the lease, not his."

"Then call your landlord and get the locks changed." She scribbled another phone number on the card. "And tomorrow call me and I'll have the name of a lawyer who can help you get a restraining order if he comes around."

"Why would you do that for me? After what happened?"

"If you found out anything about me at all," Alex said, "you know I really like being a police officer. And this is what we do, Shaylynn. We protect citizens who need help, and try to put the bad guys away. I'll talk to you soon."

Alex waited until after rush hour to make the drive to her sister's house. Nicole and Charlie lived in the suburbs south of Colfax, with neat new houses and very few trees.

Her nephew ran to greet her, and she knelt to give him a big hug.

"Hey, you're getting so tall! Have you been eating your vegetables?"

"Yep! All except broccoli. Nobody likes broccoli."

"Good point. What's for dinner?"

"Mom brought home pizza!"

"Pizza sounds great. What's your favorite kind?"

"I like lots of cheese. Like Aunt CJ does."

"She does like her cheese. She was sorry she couldn't come tonight, but she says hi and that she's bringing you a present from Georgia. It's a surprise."

"Cool!"

Nicole had plates, napkins and salad on the table when they came in.

"Wash your hands," she said automatically to Charlie. "Hi, Alex."

Charlie ran off down the hall. Alex grabbed the plastic tumblers her sister used at dinners with Charlie and filled them with ice.

"How are you holding up?" Nicole asked as she opened the pizza box. "With CJ out of town, I mean," she added.

"Well, if your question is directed toward my diet, I'm great. She left me homemade meatloaf, stuffed peppers and lasagna in convenient single-serving containers I can take from freezer to microwave. No cereal or fast food for me."

Nicole was watching her carefully.

"And otherwise?"

Alex put the tumblers on the counter and turned to face her.

"Nic, I'm fine. We talk every night. I know where she is. I know she's coming home. No flashbacks, no anxiety. The house is too quiet in the evenings, but I'm fine. Quit worrying."

"Big sister prerogative," Nicole said as Charlie came racing back down the hall with his hands before him to air dry.

Alex laughed. "But I'm the big sister."

"I was just borrowing your prerogative for the night."

"Pizza night!" Charlie exclaimed. "May I have my soda now with dinner?"

"Yes, you may," Nicole said. "Go ahead and grab it, we're ready to eat."

He opened the refrigerator and said, "May Aunt Alex have one too?"

"She might prefer something else."

"Actually root beer is fine," Alex said.

Nicole shot her a look.

"Maybe something later," Alex said. She needed to be clear-headed for this evening's after-dinner conversation.

The pizza was gooey and spicy. They talked about Nicole's job at a downtown law firm a little and about Charlie's new class at school a lot. After cleanup, Nicole brushed back his hair and said, "Since you were a homework machine this afternoon, I hear, you know what you get to do now."

Charlie fist-pumped into the air.

"Yea! Video games!"

"One hour, then time to brush your teeth and get into your pajamas. And maybe Aunt Alex will stay long enough to read the Harry Potter chapter to you tonight."

"This is an awesome evening!" Charlie said, and he raced again down the hall.

Alex said, "Does he run everywhere?"

"Pretty much," Nicole answered. "I keep wanting to tell him to store up some of that energy to use after he hits thirty-five, but it doesn't work that way, does it?"

"Sadly, no. Think it's still warm enough for us to sit on the back porch?"

"Should be. Want that drink now?"

"A very short one. I want to be sober..."

"For the drive home."

"Well, mostly for Harry Potter. I have a lot of trouble making my voice sound like Professor Snape."

They sat in lounge chairs at the far end of twilight when the last rim of orange light behind the mountains was almost gone. Alex had a tiny sip of her whiskey and felt the smoky burn all the way down into her stomach.

"So what's going on?" Nicole asked quietly. The darkness invited softer voices.

"Do you remember," Alex said, "sitting out here one evening when I told you I thought I was gay?"

"I do, very vividly. Not because I was shocked but because you seemed so reluctant to tell me."

"I was afraid of your disapproval."

"I told you at the time. You gave up everything for me after Dad was killed. All I ever wanted was for you to be happy. I knew you loved your job, I just wanted you to share your life with someone too."

How was she going to ease into this? "Nic, I have something else to tell you."

"What?" Her voice sharpened in alarm. "Are you and CJ really all right?"

"It's not CJ. We're fine, we're great. And nobody's sick. You're coming next week to the memorial dedication, right?"

"Not only that, I'm pulling Charlie out of school for it. I want him to see how proud he should be of his grandfather and of you, too. What has this got to do with anything?"

Alex took a deep breath.

"There was an article in the Colfax paper last week. My picture was in the paper and the reporter told the story about what happened to Dad."

"And?"

"And someone who read it…contacted me. I met with her today. She told me she's the one who hit him with her car all those years ago. She's the one who killed Dad."

Nicole set her drink on the glass-topped table between them with a clatter. She got up and went to the low brick fence that separated the patio from the yard and stared into the darkness for a couple of minutes.

When she spoke again, her voice was harsh.

"Did you arrest her?" Nicole asked.

"You think I should have?" Alex countered.

"I suppose not. The statute of limitations must have run out long ago. Damn it, Alex. Who was it? What did she say?"

"At the time she was a seventeen-year-old girl, living at home. And she says she wasn't drinking or using drugs that night. It was dark and raining and she never saw him."

"Yes, okay, accidents happen, I get that. But she kept driving, Alex! She just drove away and left him there!"

Alex got up and stood next to her sister. The two looked a lot alike despite the five-year age difference. The last year had aged Nicole, and at dinner Alex had seen the first strands of gray hair at her temples.

She put her arm around Nicole and answered her. "She panicked. People do, especially young people. It was wrong and she knows it. She knew it then, but how often do we do the wrong thing even when we know we shouldn't? She drove home and told her father what had happened. And he told her to tell no one else ever. He fixed the car himself."

"That's why Paul and the other officers couldn't find it."

"Yes. Her father died a few years ago, by the way, and she claims she never told anyone else. I think I believe her."

"So that's it, then. She gets to clear her conscience at our expense, and she has no penalty for killing him."

"I wouldn't say that. Nic, you should have seen her. She's your height and I bet she doesn't weigh a hundred pounds. The guilt has been eating her alive. She lives with a guy who hits her and steals for a living. She spent most of her twenties and thirties getting drunk. Now she's almost my age, and she waits tables in a pancake house and rents a tiny frame house in a less-than-great neighborhood. The court of her conscience has made her pay a thousand times over for her crime. One error in judgment, one panicked mistake in a single moment, and she not only took Dad's life, she ruined her own."

Nicole turned and looked at her. Alex could see her eyes glittering as they reflected the lights from inside the house.

"That was quite a speech," she said. "Ever think about law school?"

"I think you're all the lawyer the family needs. I told you because you have a right to know and because I'm hoping we can find a way to forgive her together. Because holding on to our resentment of her will only hurt us. You know that."

Nicole turned back toward the darkness of the yard.

"After David died, I was angry for a long time. Then I could see how it was poisoning Charlie's life and my own. David was a good man who loved us and he wouldn't want that." She exhaled and went back to her chair and her drink.

"Dad wouldn't want that either, I guess," she said.

"I don't think so either. Forgiveness, though. It's going to take some time."

"Most hard things do," Nicole said.

CHAPTER FOURTEEN

CJ's phone rang as she began another drive down Abercorn Street.

"CJ St. Clair."

"Miz St. Clair, this is Annamae Barksdale. I believe you left me a message this morning."

"Thank you for calling me back, Miz Barksdale. I have just a couple of questions for you. I don't think I'll take up more than a minute or so of your time."

"Your message said you were calling about a showing I had with Paula Prendergast on the twenty-fifth of last month."

"Yes, that's right. I'm trying to verify that she was with you on Tybee Island that evening and when she left."

There was a silence so long on the line that CJ thought the call had been dropped.

"Miz Barksdale, are you still there?"

"Yes. Yes, I'm here. I should tell you I had a conversation with Paula after you left your message."

"Did you?" CJ's curiosity kicked into overdrive.

"Yes. You see, Paula told you the story that she and I agreed upon."

"Ah. Miz Barksdale, are y'all telling me you didn't tell the police the truth?"

"Well, no. The police never called me. When I talked to Paula a bit ago, she suggested I could be candid with you about that evening."

"Please do."

"I did...see Paula that night. But we weren't on Tybee Island."

"Ah. But you were together?"

"I want you to understand, Miz St. Clair. Paula thought it might be problematic if the police knew where she actually was and what she was actually doing. So we agreed on the Tybee Island story so that they would believe it was impossible for her to have done the killing."

"Are you telling me that Paula left you before seven forty that night?"

"Not at all. We were in my condo at Bahia Bleu. Do you know where that is?"

"Yes, not far from Savannah State. What time did she leave?" The area was certainly a lot closer than Tybee Island was to St. Paul's Church.

CJ was doing the calculation in her mind of how quickly Paula could have made it to the church across town when Annamae Barksdale said, "She didn't leave. Not that night, I mean. She left around six the next morning."

"What? She spent the night, you're saying."

"Yes."

Apparently Paula wasn't lying when she said she enjoyed a change of pace from men. "She didn't leave that night? Not at all?"

"Not at all," Annamae said. Her voice was husky, but CJ couldn't tell if it was embarrassment or some other emotion she couldn't name.

"Thank you for calling me, Miz Barksdale. My advice to you and Miz Prendergast is the same: tell the police the truth. I don't think there will be any repercussions for you."

"Really? You don't know my husband, Miz St. Clair."

She ended the phone call, and CJ said aloud to no one, "In the name of all that is holy, is anybody in Chatham County keeping their marriage vows these days?"

When she arrived at the Oglethorpe Mall, she parked her car in a surface parking lot, staying far from any other cars and from the attached parking structure. Anyone hoping to sneak up on her now would have to do a sprint for fifty yards to get to her or take a sniper shot from the roof of Macy's.

She found Savannah Sweets next to JCPenney's and made her purchases. Then she walked down the mall to the designated meeting place near the food court.

Laura was waiting for her, staring into her phone.

"Hi," CJ said. "I brought treats."

Laura looked up. "Hi. What treats?"

CJ opened her treasure and displayed it.

"I thought it was time for an afternoon sweet so I bought some divinity."

Laura stared at the puffy white lumps.

"What is that? They look like little clouds."

"Oh, my dear, it's a Southern delicacy."

"Are they sweet?"

"Yes. Kind of a white fudge but without the chocolate. I think you'll like them."

Laura picked up a confection and bit into it.

"Oh my gosh," she said in midchew.

"I know." CJ grinned. "I love them."

"What are these made out of?"

"Pretty much just egg whites, corn syrup and sugar. The trick is getting them to dry properly in this humidity. It's easier in Colorado, although you have to adjust the cooking temperature because we're at altitude."

"You can make these?" Laura looked astonished.

"Of course," CJ said. "It's not that hard. I could teach you sometime, if you'd like."

"So you know how to cook? My mom didn't cook much. We did real simple stuff, like chicken. Dad pretty much grills everything or we get takeout." Her face fell into sadness.

"I'm sorry," CJ said. "I didn't mean to make you think about everything that's happened."

Laura gave her a half smile.

"It's okay. I miss her a lot."

"I know." What else could she say?

"Anyway, I was meaning to ask you if you talked to your... um, partner? Is that what you call her?"

"Yes. I'm not too fond of 'wife,' but that's what she is. Either one is fine. Her name is Alex."

"Yeah, Alex. Did you talk to her?"

"I did. We're in agreement. If your dad does end up having to go to prison, you can come to Colorado."

"Oh. That's great, really." The relief on her face and in her voice was profound. "But...what if Grandmother...um...fights with you? Like for custody, I mean."

"She might do that," CJ conceded. "But I'm not too worried. You're old enough now to say where you want to live and any judge will honor that decision unless you want to live in an unsafe place."

"But...um, what if you're not okay with the judge? I mean because you're gay."

CJ had considered this. She said, "We have some options. It's terrible that people are still prejudiced, but they are. Try not to worry about it too much. I have some money, unlike a lot of people who are discriminated against, and I won't go down without a fight. Besides," CJ added as cheerfully as she could, "I'm still working on your father's case. He may never have to see the inside of a prison."

She wrapped up the rest of the divinity and handed it to Laura.

"You can take this home. Meantime, let's do our window-shopping, okay? Where are your favorite stores?"

They spent a pleasant couple of hours strolling around the mall. Laura confessed her love of Starbucks so CJ bought coffees on the way. Finally Laura looked at her phone and sighed.

"Dad just texted me," she said. "He's on his way here to pick me up. I had a nice time, Aunt CJ."

CJ had enjoyed her time too. Laura was at heart a kind and thoughtful girl, but she did have a sharp sense of independence and a sharper tongue on occasion. CJ thought she would need some guidance in the next few years to finish growing up properly. She hoped Clayton was up to the task.

She hoped Clayton got a chance to do it.

They waited outside Macy's until Clayton pulled up. He was in a different car than CJ had seen before.

"Hey, kiddo. Get in. Any news, Belle?" He called to them from the window.

"Nothing much, but I'm working on a few things. I thought you were driving a BMW before."

"Oh, yeah. It's in the shop. This is my weekend car. Isn't she a beauty? Mercedes GT Coupe."

What the hell, Clayton? she thought. *You can't make your house payments without Mama's help and you're driving a hundred thousand dollars plus sports car.*

He always has to have the latest toys, Paula had told her.

She watched them drive off, Laura waving good-bye to her through the window.

CJ walked slowly back to her car, thinking hard. Halfway there she stopped and shook herself awake.

Don't daydream, she told herself. *You're out in public. Keep your eyes open.*

Had she seen it without it registering in her consciousness? Parked at the end of a row, as close to her rental as possible without being obvious, was a white pickup.

Of course about twenty percent of Savannah's population seemed to drive white pickups. But this one had a man in it and he was wearing a baseball cap pulled low.

On the plus side, he didn't appear to have spotted her yet. She turned between two cars as if she were going to get in one of them, then crouched down and eased herself a couple of rows away. Then she circled around until she could get a clear view of the license plate from the back.

CJ took out her cell phone and carefully punched in the number in a text message and hit send. Five minutes later her phone dinged a response.

Truck registered to Don Sharpless of Savannah. Know him?

Oh, Donny, she smiled. *I sure do.*

She responded with a quick thank-you to Frank Morelli and made a phone call. And waited right where she was.

It took a few minutes for her to hear the sirens. She watched as the back of Donny's head began to move as the sirens got closer and louder. Finally two white and blue Savannah Chatham police cars appeared in the parking lot and began screaming up the row.

CJ wondered if he'd make an attempt to bluff it out or try to see if his pickup would outrun the cruisers. What she did not expect was that he would try to lose himself in the parking lot on foot.

He slammed out of the truck and took off running. He slipped once but recovered and kept going.

If he'd known he was going to be sprinting, CJ thought, he might have swapped out those cowboy boots for some sneakers.

He had just reached what he thought was the relative safety of the cars behind him when CJ stepped out from behind a handy SUV, her gun up and pointed at his chest. In her free hand she had her Colfax PD badge prominently displayed for the officers' benefit when they joined them in a few seconds.

Donny skidded to a stop, his eyes wide with shock. Stuck in the front of his belt was what CJ assumed was a .45 semiautomatic pistol. His eyes were fastened on the barrel of her gun.

"You know I'm a police officer, Donny," CJ said. "And you are going to be under arrest in about half a minute. Hands in the air now."

He continued to stare at her. She saw his right hand twitch as he lifted it.

As always in a crisis, time slowed to slow-motion, frame by frame. Her hearing was blunted as all of her energy was channeled through her eyes, watching him, waiting for the first movement of his hand toward his gun. She kept her own hand as steady as she could and aimed her weapon at the middle of his chest.

"Don't do it, Donny. I'm a really good shot."

Perhaps he believed her. Perhaps he was just a coward.

He put his hands up high.

"Miz St. Clair," Detective Monroe said. "This is getting very tiresome. I have a few things to do during my days other than continue to show up at your crime scenes."

"Hey, if you could get people to stop stalking me with guns and leaving me threatening notes, I would be very happy to let you have your lunches and dinner in peace," CJ replied.

She was sitting in the back of a police cruiser. The front seats were pushed all the way back which failed to accommodate her long legs. Given that she couldn't exit when she wanted, she was starting to feel ever so slightly claustrophobic.

"Mr. Sharpless says you threatened to shoot him," Monroe continued.

"As he'd already tried on one occasion to shoot me and, as he was armed and fleeing your police department when we met an hour ago, I thought I was entitled to detain a fleeing felon. You're quite welcome, by the way."

"This isn't funny, Miz St. Clair," he said.

"No, it isn't," CJ responded with asperity. "It's Lieutenant St. Clair, by the way, and I'd like to make a point here. I'm on your side, Detective. If the world is good guys and bad guys, I'm one of the good guys. I know this isn't my jurisdiction and I'm trying very hard not to interfere in your case, but I'm not your enemy. I'm actually a nice person. Want to tell me what it is about me that's gotten your nose so out of joint?"

Monroe looked out the window. CJ could see a muscle working in his jaw.

"I don't like being told what to do, that's all," he said.

"When did I do that?" CJ said.

"You didn't. Somebody's got some juice, though. My chief called my boss and I was told to quote stay out of your way unquote."

"Who would…Ah, Detective. I believe I've spotted my mother's fine hand at work here. She likes to make generous contributions to various candidates and I don't doubt she made a few phone calls."

CJ leaned forward over the seat back.

"I'm sorry," she said. "Political pressure has no place in police investigations and yet it happens all the time. I want you to know I had nothing to do with this."

He continued to stare out the window, but the muscle stopped clenching.

"I'm going to have a little talk with Mama," she said. "And again, I'm sorry. Am I free to go?"

He handed back her weapon and said, "I guess I have to give you credit. You've pulled it twice but haven't used it. You must have some good training."

"Some," she conceded. "Will you let me know how it goes with Donny?"

"I'll call you tomorrow, Lieutenant St. Clair."

Charles opened the door and looked surprised.

"Miz St. Clair. Were we expecting you this evening?"

"No, we weren't, Charles. Thank you."

He didn't actually invite her into the house, but CJ came in anyway. He recovered quickly from his discomfort and said, "May I take your jacket?"

She didn't see any point in making her gun a point of curiosity.

"No, I won't be staying long," she answered. "Where is Mama?"

"She's in the library."

That confused CJ. "And where would that be?"

"I believe it used to be your father's study."

Of course. She said, "Thank you, Charles. I'd like to have a few minutes of private conversation with my mother, please."

He looked uncomfortable again but said only, "Of course, ma'am."

The bookcases were still in what had been her father's private sanctuary at the back of the house, but everything else had changed. The wood had been whitewashed and his giant mahogany desk was gone, the desk that held the big jar of caramels that CJ and her brother used to sneak in and steal. Gone from the shelves were her father's huge medical books: *Gray's Anatomy*, Hurst's *The Heart*, Schwartz's *Principles of Surgery*, *Physician's Desk Reference* and others whose names she couldn't remember. Now some of the bookcases held her mother's novels, others were filled with Hummel figurines. Where the desk had sat were two leather wing chairs with a table between them and a reading lamp. The curtains were drawn and the light was on.

Her mother sat in the yellow pool of light, upright in her chair with a book in her lap and a magnifying glass in her hand. She looked up in surprise as CJ entered.

"What are you doing here, Belle?"

"Sorry to drop in unannounced," CJ said. "Must be a family trait."

"Did you drive over here for the sole purpose of being rude?" Lydia St. Clair asked. "Or do you actually have some news to report at last?"

CJ sat down on the chair next to her mother.

"I have several items for our discussion tonight," CJ began. "First, who did you call to get the police department to leave me alone?"

She snapped the book closed with a thud.

"I know the deputy city manager and I believe he made some calls."

"You really should have told me," CJ responded. "I haven't exactly been making friends around town."

Lydia gave a delicate snort.

"That's hardly the point. The relevant question is: do you know who killed Amy?"

"It's not certain, but I helped the police arrest a man tonight I believe is connected to the case," CJ answered.

Lydia sat up straighter.

"Really? That is good news."

CJ lifted a hand.

"The police aren't sure yet and neither am I. But I think we're making some progress."

"Have you told your brother yet?"

"No. I plan to meet with him tomorrow."

"I should call him." She set the book aside and reached for the cordless telephone sitting on the table beside her.

CJ laid her hand over her mother's hand to stop her.

"Not yet," CJ said. "I still have some work to do."

"What on earth is wrong with you, Belle? Your brother needs to know as soon as possible."

"I have some other questions for you," CJ said. "Why didn't you tell me you loaned Clayton money a couple of years ago?"

Lydia waved the question away. "I hardly see the relevance of that."

"Really, Mama? Because it's directly related to Clayton's motive. He supposedly killed Amy for the insurance money. Didn't you think saving him from a bankruptcy filing was information relevant to the case?"

"It didn't matter. Right before all this happened Clayton told me his money troubles were all going to be over very soon. So he would have no reason to kill Amy."

"My God! Mama, don't you see? That sounds as if his solution to his money troubles *was killing Amy*!"

"So there was no point in telling you any of it. It wouldn't help Clayton, it would only hurt."

CJ stood up. She had to pace or she was going to start screaming.

"This is about finding the truth, Mama! Not about shielding Clayton from the consequences of his actions. Don't you understand that? I would never be part of concealing evidence. I told you that in the beginning."

Lydia leaned back in her chair. The half of her face away from the light was in shadow; the other half was twisted in a mask of disapproval so sharp that CJ could almost feel it pierce her like a shard of glass.

"'How sharper than a serpent's tooth it is to have a thankless child,'" Lydia murmured.

"Thanks for the *King Lear*, Mama. Now I have one more question for you."

CJ put her hands on either side of the arms of her mother's chair and leaned into her, trapping her.

"What did I do to make you hate me?" CJ asked.

Lydia St. Clair tightened her mouth.

"You know what you are."

"You're going to claim you hate me because I'm a lesbian, is that it? Well, I'm not buying it, so try again. In my whole life I never remember that you liked me for even one day. Years before I came out to you, you treated me like a 'thankless child.' Before I go home I want you to tell me why."

"You're being absurd." Lydia spat the words at her.

"No, I'm not. You know it's true. Answer the question."

Lydia looked away and her lips seemed to disappear. From two feet away CJ could see every line and wrinkle from her mother's lifetime spent in hoarding disapproval.

CJ knew with sudden clarity that she would never see her mother again. It was now or never.

"Tell me, Mama."

"You want to know? Fine, I'll tell you. You were never the daughter I should have had. I couldn't believe I actually bore you. From the beginning you were loud and precocious, always going where you didn't belong. You spent half your girlhood in the kitchen with the black cook, for pity's sake! Or you were outside, playing with boys, always getting dirty. You never wanted to learn anything I had to teach you, but your father! Oh, he could do no wrong! You followed him around when he was home and when he wasn't you'd climb into his chair and pretend to read his books. Medical texts! You had no interest in clothes or your hair or behaving yourself like a lady. You wouldn't date suitable young men, you wanted to be out with your friends doing God knows what! You were always a great disappointment to me, Belle. I shouldn't have been surprised when you told me you were a homosexual because God knows you were never a lady, never a good daughter, never a proper woman at all! Does that answer your question?"

Her words were meant to wound, to maim. CJ waited a moment for the agony to begin.

But all she felt was a sting like the scrape on her hand. The pain was there, but she knew she would survive it. Because nothing was really a surprise. She'd known every word of truth all along. Her mother had shown her for years.

CJ leaned back and unbuttoned the top two buttons of her blouse. In the light from the lamp her scar was a thin white line but clearly visible, she knew.

Lydia's eyes went to it. "What is that? Did you have heart surgery?"

"Yes," CJ said. "Because someone shot me in the chest and almost killed me."

Lydia's eyes narrowed. "What are you..."

"I was in the hospital a long time and it took even longer to recover after I went home," CJ said. "There was a lot of pain and weakness, but I lived through it, Mama. I lived and everything was better at the end of it. And I know you wanted to hurt me just now, but I want you know I'm going to live through this too.

"It doesn't actually hurt that much, as it turns out. Good-bye, Mother."

CJ left the room and didn't look back.

CHAPTER FIFTEEN

CJ slept in because she could and because she was exhausted. She called for coffee and fruit to be sent upstairs, and then she took a long hot shower designed to wash away Savannah from her skin.

Her cell phone rang as she finished drying her hair. Humidity insured that process took about twice as long here as it did in Colorado.

"Detective Monroe, nice to hear from you."

"Lieutenant. It's not too early, I hope."

"Not at all." CJ sat on the edge of the bed. "I hope you had a productive evening."

"And a productive morning as well," he answered. "We've had a nice talk with Mr. Sharpless and with Melissa St. Clair as well, who was kind enough to join us last night."

Was the case over? CJ could only hope.

"And were they talking to you?" CJ asked.

"Eventually. We got several versions of events over the course of time, but you know how that goes."

"Yes, I do. Have you gotten a final version?"

"I think so. The short story is that Donny Sharpless was responsible for the shooting in the parking garage. Melissa wrote the note and delivered it to your hotel. Her fingerprint matches the unidentified one we found on the letter. They had obviously planned the incidents together. Sharpless says he was just going to threaten you yesterday, by the way. He claims he had no intent to injure you."

"And do we believe that?"

"We do not. After the prior shooting incident, the DA has decided on a charge of attempted murder with various assorted other weapons and assault charges. Melissa was not happy to be charged with being an accessory, and we will be adding a resisting arrest charge to the list. She scratched up one of my guys pretty good. I doubt she's in a better mood this morning after a night in jail."

"Other than general hostility toward me, did they tell you what the motive might have been?"

Monroe made a noise that might have been a chuckle if he'd had a sense of humor.

"It's pretty out there, but they are, and excuse the terminology, a pair of really dumb crackers. Melissa got it in her head that if Clayton were convicted, this would somehow mean that she'd be entitled to all of his worldy goods in the property settlement. And she really wanted the house, I guess. Anyway, they probably would have trouble hitting triple digits on an IQ test if we added the scores together. They thought that if they could get you to stop looking around that Clayton would be found guilty. And that's it."

CJ's heart sank. "You're telling me they didn't have anything to do with Amy's murder in the first place?"

He cleared his throat.

"We spent a lot of time on that. They gave me the same alibi, that they were together alone all night. But this time they remembered something important."

"What was that?"

"Pizza," he said.

"Pizza?"

"They ordered pizza delivered. And we tracked down the delivery guy this morning and he identified both of them from a photo lineup. The time on the delivery order confirms that he actually handed them a large sausage and pepperoni at Melissa's apartment at eight oh seven p.m. the night of the murder. Neither one of them could have been at St. Paul's that night shooting Melissa. They didn't do the murder."

CJ wanted to throw the cell phone across her hotel room. Instead she said, "I want to thank you for calling me, Detective. And for all your hard work. I'll be in touch."

"Good-bye," he said, his voice almost apologetic.

After that disappointment, it was time for a special treat, CJ decided. Clayton suggested lunch and she was in the mood for something really bad for her diet and good for her psyche.

They met at Your Mama's Chicken & Waffles not far from Clayton's office. The restaurant itself was one step up from being a joint, but it was clean and the smells alone transported CJ close to heaven.

Clayton didn't need a menu to order the crab rice. CJ had come for fried chicken and waffles and nothing else would do.

"Longer lunch period today?" CJ asked him.

Clayton shrugged.

"I had a couple of cancellations. Not that unusual. Preston probably told you a few people have dropped us or switched to him. It's no big deal. When this is over, they'll come back or new patients will take their place."

Today he was wearing a pale pink oxford cloth dress shirt, but he'd taken off his tie if he'd been wearing one and his sleeves were unbuttoned and rolled up to mid-forearms. He looked tired and CJ wondered how well he'd been sleeping.

CJ folded her hands on the table.

"I have some things to tell you," she said. "And I have a question for you too. Are you up for this?"

"Sure. Have you found something?"

"I think so. First I should tell you that Missy and her new boyfriend spent last night in the Chatham County Jail."

"They what?"

CJ outlined everything she knew about the case against them. As she finished, their food arrived. Nestled on top of a crispy waffle that covered her plate was a golden brown fried chicken breast. CJ regarded it for a happy moment, then poured maple syrup over waffle and chicken both. Then she picked up her knife and fork.

Clayton was shaking his head.

"Missy was never the brightest stem in the bouquet," he said, "but I didn't think she was that stupid."

"Detective Monroe seemed rather surprised too, although if you work on the job long enough you eventually stop being shocked at just how stupid criminals can be." She hesitated for a moment before adding, "The bad news is they had nothing to do with Amy's murder."

Clayton stopped with a forkful of rice and crab halfway to his mouth.

"What? But I thought…"

CJ shook her head.

"They have an alibi. Detective Monroe checked. Neither one of them could have done it."

He put the fork down with the bite untaken.

"I guess I never really thought she was a killer, but dammit, Belle! We're no closer than we were before."

"I wouldn't say that," CJ said. "I went to visit Mama last evening."

"Of your own accord? Hard to believe."

"It wasn't a pleasant conversation. But she did mention something I wanted to ask you about."

He seemed suddenly wary.

"What was that?"

"Why did you tell her you thought your money troubles would soon be over?"

"Oh, that. Well, the practice is going so well Pres and I have been talking about taking on another orthodontist and…"

"You're lying, Clayton, and you're doing it badly. I talked to Preston, remember? If things don't turn around pretty quickly, I suspect he's either going to have to dissolve the partnership or you're both filing Chapter Eleven bankruptcy. Try again."

His wariness turned to sullenness. He pressed his lips together, and CJ had a jolt of discomfort at watching her mother's expression appear on her brother's face.

"This doesn't have anything to do with Amy's murder," he said.

"It does and if you think it doesn't, then you're fooling yourself."

CJ laid her knife and fork down across her plate. The waitress came to remove it and looked questioningly at Clayton's half-eaten food.

"Are you finished, sir?"

He waved the food away and she picked up both plates.

CJ smiled at her and said, "Mine was delicious, thanks."

When she was gone, CJ said, "I've talked to a lot of people over the last ten days or so. One of them said something interesting about you. Want to hear it?"

"I'm guessing you're not going to give me a choice."

"You're right. Somebody told me you always had to be seeing at least two women at the same time. From what I know of you, that sounds about right. Care to comment?"

"What is the point of this? You know I have a roving eye, it's no secret."

"You've been seeing Tayla for, what, nine months or so? And you broke up with Missy in March. Six months is a long time for you to go without cheating on Tayla too."

"Belle, this is ridiculous."

"You sound a lot like Mama, Clayton. If I say something she doesn't want to hear, she tells me I'm being silly or absurd."

That shut him up as she suspected it would. His face returned to its sullen expression.

"So then I asked myself: who could you possibly be seeing on the side who might also be the solution to your money problems? The obvious answer, of course, is a wealthy woman.

That was certainly a possibility. Are you having an affair with a rich woman, Clayton?"

"Of course not."

"No, you're not. Because you were having an affair with Amy."

His face lost all color. He seemed unable to deny the allegation or unable to speak at all. She didn't need his words to verify her conclusion.

"I've spent quite a while looking for Amy's mystery beau, and it turns out you were making up with your ex-wife," CJ continued. "I didn't know you owned a sports car until last night. Both Laura and a neighbor told me they heard a sports car leaving Amy's house in the months before she was killed on evenings when Laura thought her mother might have a date. It was you, trying to get her back."

He still seemed struck dumb.

CJ said, "If you and Amy got remarried, things would get much easier, wouldn't they? Amy could still work and you wouldn't be paying her maintenance anymore. And your child support payments would go away too. That's a lot of help for your monthly cash flow. It would cost a lot less for the three of you to live together, especially with Amy's income, than it would for you to make those payments. No wonder you told Mama your financial situation was looking optimistic. All you had to do was seal the deal with Amy and everything was much better."

Clayton threw down his napkin and shoved his chair back with a loud screech on the floor. He jumped up and stalked out the door.

CJ caught the waitress's eye and threw a couple of bills onto the table. Then she went after him.

He was standing outside in the parking lot beside his Mercedes coupe. He had one hand on it as if to ask why it had betrayed him.

CJ said, "Clayton."

He turned on her.

"That's what you think, isn't it? That I went after Amy because of the money? Well, you don't know any fucking thing about it, Belle. Not one fucking thing."

CJ stood still.

"Then tell me, Clayton," she said.

He slumped back against the hood of his car.

"I've screwed up so many times," he said. "Any pretty girl, any nice ass and I was all over it. I really like women, I do. I like chasing them and I like catching them. I just never liked keeping them for long.

"But I kept making lousy choices. Paula, Missy and a half-dozen girls you don't even know about in between. I could never get it right. And then after Missy, I just..."

"You found Tayla."

"I like Tayla, I really do. But she's not special, only another girl, another woman to catch and release." He sighed. "I could see it in people's eyes. 'What's wrong with you?' Laura was old enough now to wonder what the hell kind of man I am. I was certainly starting to wonder what the hell kind of man I am. I thought about it a long time. And I realized I'd gotten it right the first time. The only one of them I ever really cared for was Amy."

CJ could hear the grief in his voice. "Oh, Clayton."

"I went to her. I told her I'd been an idiot. If Paula hadn't called Amy all those years ago, hell, the affair would have blown over eventually. I might still have been married to Amy. Anyway, I asked Amy if I could prove to her that I was worth another chance. She was really reluctant, but I was willing to take my time. We were just starting to get it back, Belle. She was starting to trust me a little bit and I knew she'd never really fallen out of love with me. If we'd only had more time..."

He broke down and CJ went to him. He sobbed on her shoulder as she held him. Passersby going to their cars glanced curiously at them, but CJ held on tight. She could feel her blouse getting damp with his tears.

He stopped after a few minutes, using his palms to wipe away the wetness on his cheeks.

"I'm sorry, Belle. So sorry. I never really cried for her."

"You could have told me, Clayton."

"You have to understand. I loved her, Belle. I always loved her. I would never, ever have hurt her. But I knew how it would look to the police. They'd say I was using her, that I killed her because she broke up with me or something. I didn't tell anybody, not Laura, not Mama. I couldn't tell you. I didn't know how."

"I understand, Clayton. I do. And I want you to know how very sorry I am."

"This doesn't help you at all, does it?"

"Actually, it might. I have a call to make and maybe a meeting. I'll call you later this afternoon. Okay?"

"Okay. Belle? I'm sorry. I should have told you."

"You should have. But I think maybe it's going to be all right."

She recognized Linn Childs's SUV as it pulled into the parking lot at St. Paul's. This time she went to greet Linn as she got out of the truck.

"It was really good of you to come and meet me again. I know it was hard on you last time," CJ said to her.

Linn said, "Well, you've made it easy for me. It's an easy stop on my way to pick up the kids. You said it would take five minutes?"

"Yes, but it might be difficult for you. I need to re-create something that happened on the night Amy was killed."

Linn looked a bit tentative but said, "Okay. What do you need?"

CJ led her to the spot on the curb where the shooting took place.

"I'm going to get a hoodie out of my car," she said. "Is that okay?"

Linn nodded reluctantly.

CJ grabbed the gray hooded sweatshirt she'd bought an hour ago at the Goodwill store and slipped it on. It occurred to her that the murderer might have bought their own hoodie at the same place, finding one that looked like Clayton's jacket. She pulled the hood on over her head and stepped over near Linn.

"Is this about the right distance?" she asked.

"Yes. Maybe one step closer."

CJ got nearer and Linn inhaled sharply.

"I'm sorry," CJ said. "If this is too difficult, we can stop."

"No. No, I'm all right."

"I want you to replay the movie, okay? Look carefully. Is the height right?"

"Yes. Very close."

"Good. Now here's my shoulder bag. Did Amy have it on her shoulder?"

"Yes."

"Okay. Now he pointed the gun at her and said, 'Purse.' And she handed it to him. So do that for me."

Linn took the purse off her shoulder by the straps and handed it to CJ.

"Now tell me again what he did."

"He put the strap on over his left shoulder," Linn said.

CJ did it. "Like that? He didn't fumble with it? You're sure he didn't just hold it?"

"No, I'm sure. Exactly like you did."

"You're doing really well. Now, one more thing. I'm going to run away and I want you to watch me carefully. I want to see if it looks like the run you saw that night."

"Yes. Okay. I'm ready."

CJ turned and made her run across the parking lot. She was perspiring in the heat with the sweatshirt on by the time she walked back to Linn.

It was the most animated she'd ever seen Linn.

"That was it!" she exclaimed. "That's what I saw!"

"Are you sure?" CJ asked.

"I'm sure. How did you figure it out?"

"Lots of work," CJ said. "I'm very grateful to you, Miz Childs, for all your help. You can go and pick up your kids now."

"Have you solved it?" Linn asked.

"Yes," CJ answered. "I've solved it."

CHAPTER SIXTEEN

CJ expected Clayton at her hotel around five thirty, after work. She decided a bottle of wine was a good idea and had a bottle of chardonnay delivered. She wedged it into her ice bucket to chill and left it on the table behind the tiny sofa in her suite.

She'd talk to Clayton first, but her next phone call was to Detective Monroe, the last one she'd be making to him, she hoped.

CJ walked into the bedroom and glanced at the bedside clock to see if she would have time to change, take off her jacket and her gun. Maybe she should even put on a fresh blouse after her wind sprint in the parking lot at St. Paul's in the humid ninety-degree heat. Then she heard the knock on her door. Clayton was early.

I guess no changing clothes for me, she thought, and she went to answer the door.

When she opened it, all she could see was the gun muzzle pointed at her head.

"You're going to die."

The world fell away from her. In the next moment the flash from the barrel would be her last sight. She would probably never even hear the explosion of the gunshot.

No, she could control that last second, she thought. She closed her eyes a moment and called up Alex in her mind, the blue denim eyes sparkling at her, the smell of her sandalwood skin, the low murmur of her voice in CJ's ear. That would be her last thought on earth, that memory. She wished she could tell Alex that her last moment had been filled only with her.

I love you, darlin'. I'm sorry.

"You're going to die if you don't back up very quietly."

CJ opened her eyes again and took two steps backward.

"Turn around."

Going into the bedroom? Or am I about to be shot in the head?

Then there was a terrible moment of pain before darkness.

Sound came back first. Voices. Had she left the television on? The radio?

Not the television. A conversation. A man and a woman. Pain radiated through her head from the base of her skull. She dug her hands into something soft. Carpeting tugged at her fingertips.

Okay. On the floor. I hit my head. What happened?

Memory came back in a trickle. *No, I didn't hit my head*, she thought. *There was a gun.*

Had she been shot? CJ tried to think, to remember. Had she heard a gunshot? She couldn't recall hearing one. Would she have heard it?

Part of her wanted to lie on this nice soft floor forever because the slightest movement caused searing agony through the top of her head. *Might be a gunshot wound*, she thought again.

No. She hit me.

She tried cracking open her eyes slightly. Not too far away on the carpet lay something dark green. Her attempts to focus were difficult, but eventually she recognized it.

Wine bottle. The chardonnay. She hit me with the wine bottle. Probably didn't want to risk hitting me with the gun.

That was all she could do for now. She closed her eyes and lay motionless, trying to will the pain in her head to abate.

She concentrated on the voices.

"…doesn't matter now," the woman was saying. "Don't you understand? I took care of it. Now we can get married."

"I told you on the phone we're through," the man said.

Clayton. Be careful, Clayton. She has a gun.

The woman laughed and it was an unpleasant sound that hurt CJ's ears.

"You're confused," the woman said. "I committed murder for you. We're never going to be through, don't you see?"

"Okay. Okay. But I need to help Belle, all right? She needs an ambulance."

"Will you stop talking about your bitch of a sister? Everything I did, I did for you. She was interfering in the plan, don't you see that? Now we can leave."

She couldn't let them leave, CJ thought. Clayton was in terrible danger.

CJ wondered if she could even stand up. She opened her eyes again.

She was lying behind the couch. She rolled slightly over from her stomach to see where the people were in the room.

Clayton was sitting in the chair across from the couch. The woman was pacing up and down with her back to CJ most of the time.

If I can just get to my knees and draw my weapon…

She could still feel the gun on her hip. Slowly she reached back and eased the revolver from her holster, trying to move her head as little as possible as she did so. Even the slightest movement was agony and it was compounded by blurred vision and a sudden wave of nausea.

They were still talking, but she was hardly listening. All CJ could do was try to think. She was afraid to take action while Clayton was in the line of fire but more afraid not to. As soon as she stood up, even partially, the woman couldn't help but see her.

She looked at the wine bottle and considered a distraction. Could she throw it? It was only a good idea in the abstract. CJ seriously doubted if she could even lift it and toss it at all without throwing up, much less throw it across the room with any accuracy.

She was going to have to draw on the woman and pray that she could get her to surrender before CJ passed out again.

Give me the strength to do this.

CJ tried moving her head experimentally. The pain was still there but at least it wasn't any worse. She was going to have to do this now or lose her chance.

Somehow she pushed up from the floor and staggered to her feet. The room wobbled around her.

She blinked to get her vision to steady. Her gun was up and ready.

Clayton saw her first and froze.

As the woman began to turn around, CJ yelled, "Put your gun down right now, Tayla!"

Tayla stood frozen, but she still had the gun in her hand. She was facing Clayton and she lifted it toward him.

"You put your gun down or I'll kill him."

CJ tried to breathe. The act of staying on her feet took an exercise of will so strong she hardly had time for aiming her weapon.

"I know you're under a lot of pressure here," CJ said in a calmer tone. "So take a second to think. You said you loved Clayton. You really want him to die after all you put yourself through?"

"I…" Her voice shook. "I will kill him!"

"Tayla. Listen to me. If you fire the gun, no one will ever understand why you did it. No one will ever know. You won't have a chance to tell anyone your story. No defense, no explanation to a jury, no chance for an acquittal or an appeal."

"What?" Tayla's voice sounded genuinely puzzled. Clayton was staring at CJ with wide eyes.

"Put the gun down and no one will hurt you," CJ said. The room was starting to weave in and out and she wasn't sure how much longer she could keep talking. "If you don't put the gun down, if you try to shoot my brother, it's over."

"What are you going to do?" Tayla seemed to have regained her footing. "Shoot me in the back? You're a cop, you won't do that."

"Yes, I will. If you take a shot at Clayton, I will blow the back of your head to kingdom come. No jury, no temporary insanity, no appeal. You'll be dead before you hit the floor."

"You're not going to do that," Tayla said, sounding less sure of herself.

"You're wrong and you're gambling with your life. Don't take that chance because I'm thinking about shooting you anyway in about two seconds. Now put the damn gun on the floor."

The ultimatum hung in the air and CJ knew she was almost out of time.

Tayla's shoulders dropped in defeat. She leaned down and laid the pistol on the carpet.

"Turn around and face me," CJ said. "Hands in the air."

She complied and gave CJ a sneer.

"Clayton, get the gun," CJ ordered him crisply. "Do you know how to use it?"

"Well enough," Clayton said.

"Good. Stand well away from her and if she moves, shoot her."

"You don't look so good," Tayla said to CJ.

"Don't worry about me," CJ said. "It only takes about twelve pounds of pressure to pull the trigger on this gun and I've got just about the right amount of strength left."

CJ awkwardly fumbled with her cell phone and punched in 911.

A soft beeping sound woke CJ from sleep. Her head ached, but this time she seemed to be lying in a bed on her back rather than on the floor.

She cracked open her eyes. The room lights were dimmed, and she saw the white board at the foot of her bed with the name of her nurse written on it. Hospital, then.

She risked opening her eyes all the way. In the chair near her bed was the best healing remedy she could have asked for.

"Alex," she said. Her voice came out as a croak.

Alex was standing over her at once.

"Hey, sweetheart. Water?"

"Yes, please."

She manipulated the covered plastic mug with its attached flexible straw near CJ's mouth and CJ got several sips before leaning back.

"How do you feel?" Alex asked her.

"Um. Would you be surprised to hear I have a headache?"

Alex managed a small smile. To CJ's blurry vision in the dim light, Alex looked tired and worn.

"Sorry," CJ said in a whisper.

"Don't apologize. And don't worry. I'm here now."

"Come here then."

Alex put her head all the way down next to CJ's on the pillow. CJ turned her head slightly and put her nose in Alex's neck in the soft spot just behind the angle of her jaw. She inhaled the scent of sandalwood and Alex and smiled against Alex's skin.

"Better?" Alex asked.

"I need one more thing," CJ said.

Alex leaned in and kissed her tenderly.

"Much better now," CJ said. "I thought maybe you were a dream."

"I'm really here. Where else would I be?" Alex said.

"What day is it?"

"It's been twenty-four hours more or less. You fainted after the paramedics got to the hotel so you were admitted for observation."

"Concussion."

"Yes."

CJ closed her eyes.

"She hit me with a damn bottle of chardonnay."

Alex made a noise and CJ opened her eyes again to look at her.

"What?"

"She's fortunate I wasn't the first on the scene," Alex said grimly. "That's all."

"I hope Tayla is locked up right now."

Alex sat down again and took her hand.

"You want to talk about this now?"

CJ fumbled with the adjustment on the bed and Alex helped her to sit up a bit.

"I think I do," CJ said. "Is Clayton all right?"

"I talked to him a couple of hours ago. He was here all night until I could get here late this morning."

"More damage to the Gold Card," CJ said.

"I was prepared to drive for twenty-four hours straight if necessary, but the airplane seemed faster."

"Good choice," CJ said. "Alex, I'm sorry."

"For what, sweetheart?"

"For you having to get a phone call from Clayton. It must have scared the living daylights out of you."

"It was scary," Alex conceded. "But you'll be all right eventually."

"Eventually?"

"Honey, concussions are essentially brain damage. It might take weeks or months for you to feel fully recovered. And until then we are under doctor's orders for you to take it easy."

"Okay," CJ said in a subdued voice. "When will they let me go home?"

"Tomorrow, if your symptoms have improved. Home, in this case, is back to the East Bay Inn. No flying for a few days. I dropped my bag at your hotel."

CJ shut her eyes again.

"Well, I was hoping to show you Savannah, but not exactly this way."

Alex squeezed her hand.

"I'll look forward to it."

"So tell me," CJ said, "what we know about Tayla Morrison."

Alex sat back.

"She confessed. In fact, according to Detective Monroe, with whom I had a very long telephone discussion earlier this afternoon, she wouldn't shut up. He said she acted like she was afraid no one was going to hear the full story."

"I might have had something to do with that. She shot Amy because Clayton was dating Amy again, didn't she?"

"So she says. She was apparently under the delusion that Clayton was just fooling around with Amy and that she, Tayla, was his true love. So she eliminated the competition. And helped out Clayton's financial position at the same time."

"The tragedy is that it was the other way around," CJ said. "Tayla was the fling, it was Amy whom Clayton loved all along. Awful for Laura, awful for him."

"Clayton feels pretty guilty that he triggered the confrontation in the hotel room by calling Tayla to break it off with her. And speaking of Laura, they wouldn't let her in to visit you. I met her downstairs and promised I would give you her love. Maybe we can have her come to the hotel in a day or two and see you."

"Poor kid. But at least she's not losing her father to prison."

"No, as soon as the paperwork is done they'll release Clayton's bail and dismiss the charges. Tayla said she stole the gun from her ex-husband. She knew it was one of the ones he'd bought from a guy somewhere in a bar, not a registered transaction. That's why they couldn't trace it. Ray Morrison didn't even know it was missing."

"She knew about Clayton's hooded jacket and easily got a similar one. And it was no trouble for her to put the gun in his car. But the question is: why would she frame Clayton? If she killed Amy to be with him, why was she trying to get him sent to prison?"

Alex shook her head. CJ wondered how long it would be before she would be able to perform the same action without pain.

"That's the weirdest part of this whole thing," Alex said. "According to Monroe, it was actually part of her plot to make sure Clayton stayed with her. She figured when Amy was killed that Clayton would be the prime suspect anyway, so she set him up so she could rescue him later."

"This is making my headache worse," CJ complained. "How in blue blazes was she going to do that?"

"By giving him an alibi," Alex said. "She told Monroe that she was going to break down on the witness stand and claim that Clayton had been with her all evening the night of Amy's murder. Her story was going to be that she didn't want her soon-to-be ex-husband to know and that's why she gave police false information."

"You're not serious, Alex."

"That's what she said. She actually looked up that she could afford a conviction for giving false information to the police so long as she didn't commit perjury. Probation, probably, and from her perspective Clayton would be eternally grateful and in her clutches forever."

"Her husband Ray told me she was a manipulator," CJ said. "It's hard to imagine anyone being quite that devious."

"It might have worked," Alex said. "Except that you were on the case. Care to tell me how you figured it out?"

"Once I worked out that Amy's secret boyfriend was Clayton, it wasn't hard. Tayla had the best motive then. It was just a matter of verifying that the shooter was a woman rather than a man."

"And that's the part I'm fuzzy on. How did you do that?"

"Two things. I talked to the eyewitness again and she gave me two clues. First, have you ever seen a man put a woman's purse on his shoulder? If he has to hold it, he grabs the straps or he holds it by the main section of the bag. No guy would sling the purse over his shoulder without fumbling it. It took me a while to remember that."

"Impressive." Alex smiled. "What was the other hint?"

"The eyewitness said the shooter ran away oddly. Not with a limp or in a pattern, only that there was something different about it. Women do look different from men while they're running, especially from the back. Small things, but I thought it confirmed that Tayla was our suspect. I was going to tell Clayton and urge him to break it off with her. At a minimum, I figured we had enough information for his attorney to raise some solid doubt at the trial. I just didn't anticipate she'd show up and clonk me on the head. What was she going to do?"

"She figured she and Clayton could still execute her original plan if he could get you out of the picture. I guess she thought he could talk you out of going after her."

"She really was delusional," CJ said.

"For sure. But remember in her mind Clayton truly loved only her and would do anything for her, especially after she committed a murder for his benefit. From her point of view, the plan made some kind of sense, I suppose."

"Not much. Anyway, I'm wondering if I can get some more drugs now. My head is really killing me."

"Poor brave girl. I'll go find a nurse."

Alex leaned down again for a brush of lips. "I'll be right back."

"Oh, Alex?"

"Yes, sweetheart?"

"I don't suppose you've heard anything from my mother."

"I'm sorry, CJ. She hasn't been by or called that I know of. Were you expecting her?"

No, CJ thought, *I wasn't really expecting anything from her.*

CHAPTER SEVENTEEN

"Yes, this memorial honors not only the men and women who gave their lives in the performance of their duty to their neighbors but also reminds us of something that is both vitally important and easy to forget: that our safety and our freedoms are bought with the sacrifice of others. For some people, their willingness to put on the uniforms of our country and our communities requires them to pay the highest price. For those people who serve and sacrifice we must be always grateful. May this memorial be our reminder, a symbol of our gratitude and a tribute to that sacrifice."

Alex sat down to applause. The dais had a handful of dignitaries including city council members, Paul Duncan and most of the Colfax PD command staff. She suspected the applause was in direct proportion to the brevity of her speech. She remembered that Lincoln had said in a speech that "the world will little note, nor long remember what we say here" and while that had not proven true for the Gettysburg Address, she assumed it was true of every other speech ever given on occasions like this.

But her speech didn't matter. The memorial, a slab of granite shining in the late September sun, had names engraved on it in black letters. Included was Sergeant Charles Alexander Ryan and his name would be there for a very long time. Perhaps someday Charlie, who was sitting solemnly in the audience with Nicole beside him, would show his own children the name and be proud of his legacy.

Charlie was what mattered, and Nicole and every one of the hundred or so people that sat in the hard folding chairs to honor those who had died.

In the last row sat Shaylynn Goetz. She had come in late and sat alone. Alex saw her dabbing at her eyes with a tissue.

What was she feeling? Alex could only guess. For Alex, it was the last closing of the book on her father's life, all the questions answered and laid to rest. He had died doing his job and who was to say that it had been unalloyed tragedy? From his death Alex had found her own path and that path had taken her to everything good.

Her path had taken her to CJ, who was sitting in the front row of the audience. Her own eyes were glistening, but she was smiling too. She had insisted that she was well enough to travel and that they were not going to miss this day.

The weather was all the glory of a Colorado fall. The aspen tree leaves were going golden and the slightest breeze caused the rustling sound Alex loved. The sun on her back was warm and as the dignitaries mingled with the crowd, shaking hands, she went to CJ.

"That was great, sweetheart." CJ hugged her. "You should give more speeches."

"Hardly," Alex said dryly. "That was the longest three minutes of my life."

Nicole and Charlie joined them. Charlie said, "You did real good, Aunt Alex."

"Thanks, Charlie. Your mom has always been better at making speeches than I am."

"I know. She likes to talk a lot."

"What?" Nicole exclaimed as Alex and CJ laughed.

Alex saw Shaylynn walking back slowly toward the parking lot. Alex said to Nicole, "I think there's someone you should meet."

Nicole met her eyes.

"Do I?" she asked.

"It's up to you," Alex said.

After a moment of hesitation, Nicole said, "Maybe I do."

To CJ, Alex said, "We'll be back in a second."

CJ smiled. "Come on, Charlie," she said, taking his hand. "Let's go look at your grandfather's name on the memorial."

"Okay! Aunt CJ, did you know we have the same first name?"

"Yes, I did know that."

"Do you know what Charlie told me when we were looking at the memorial?" CJ asked Alex later that evening. They were out of uniform and had their feet—and wineglasses—propped up on the coffee/wine table.

"No, what?"

"He told me he wanted to be a policeman too when he grows up."

Alex shook her head. "He's ten. We were wearing all that shiny gold stuff on our uniforms. Half the kids in Colfax probably want to be cops, the other half firefighters."

"Maybe," CJ said reluctantly. "But he looks up to you Alex. He hears stories about his grandfather and he sees his aunt. It's bound to have a lot of influence on him."

"Both aunts," Alex said, leaning over to kiss her. "God, I'm glad you're home."

"Me too. I'm sorry you didn't really get to see the city."

"What I did see was beautiful. Very different from Colorado. We'll go back."

"We will. But we won't be seeing my mother."

"I am so sorry, sweetheart. She's…I just don't have any words."

"You don't need any. It is what it is. I'm sorry for her. But the choices were hers to make and she made them. But on the bright side," she added, "I've got Laura and I've got my brother back. We talked about Christmas a little."

"Whatever you want," Alex said. "How are you feeling?"

"I'm fine. Why? You have that 'we have to talk' tone of voice."

Alex took a fortifying sip of wine.

"Have you thought any more about my applying for the chief of police job? Paul kept giving me the stink eye at the memorial service. I'm surprised he's not over here now trying to talk you—and me—into it."

"When's your actual deadline?"

"Applications are due on Friday," Alex answered.

"I think you should try," CJ said. "It's what you want. It's what I want for you. We always knew this might happen."

Alex looked at her steadily. "I don't want to advance my career at the expense of yours," Alex said. "It's not more important for me to be chief of police than it is for you to continue to advance, if that's what you want."

"I want you to do this," CJ said firmly. "We know you might not get it anyway, and if that's the case, we're fine where we are. And if you do…"

"What?"

"I really enjoyed being out in the field when I was home," CJ said. "I miss talking to people who aren't mostly cops all the time. Maybe this is a chance for me to get out of Internal Affairs. There's a lot less actual investigating in IA than I like to do. I was thinking about a change anyway."

"I'm not sure I believe you," Alex said.

"Well, you should. We still have a couple of days. Let's sleep on it and we can talk more tomorrow."

"You want to go to bed? It's a little early for you, isn't it?"

"Normally, I would agree. But I would like to go to bed now. Although I'm not really particularly sleepy."

"How is that headache, truly?" Alex asked.

"It's really most sincerely gone. No blurry vision, no wooziness, no nausea. I'm fit as a fiddle and ready for love."

Alex laughed.

"You're always so subtle," Alex said. "Would you like to make love, sweetheart?"

"Why yes, darlin'. I believe I would."

Bella Books, Inc.

Women. Books. Even Better Together.

P.O. Box 10543
Tallahassee, FL 32302

Phone: 800-729-4992
www.bellabooks.com